TO
CAMILLA SAW THE DOOR OPENING.

It opened a fraction and then stopped. Quickly, without conscious thought, she put up a hand and flicked off the light switch. She listened but all was silent.

"You come one step nearer," she said, "and I'll scream my head off."

There was complete silence.

"Who the hell are you, anyway? And how did you get in?"

Even as she spoke she knew the answer. "You're someone who knew my husband," she said with sudden knowledge. "Someone who knows me. God, who are you?"

The thought stiffened her and anger burned in her stomach. She flipped on the light.

It was very much closer than she had realised, standing by her shoulder, its paper face turned to hers. She tried to scream, but her throat was immediately constricted by the hands. Soft thick padded hands which pressed deep. And deeper.

Murder Ink.® Mysteries

Scene Of The Crime® Mysteries

A Scene Of The Crime®Mystery

A COFFIN
FROM THE PAST

Gwendoline Butler

A DELL BOOK

Published by
Dell Publishing Co., Inc.
1 Dag Hammarskjold Plaza
New York, New York 10017

This work was first published in Great Britain
by Geoffrey Bles Ltd.

Dell ® TM 681510, Dell Publishing Co., Inc.

ISBN: 0-440-11590-6

Printed in the United States of America
First U.S.A. printing—November 1982

A Scene Of The Crime®Mystery

A COFFIN FROM THE PAST

Gwendoline Butler

A DELL BOOK

Published by
Dell Publishing Co., Inc.
1 Dag Hammarskjold Plaza
New York, New York 10017

This book is fiction. All characters and incidents are
entirely imaginary.

This work was first published in Great Britain
by Geoffrey Bles Ltd.

Dell ® TM 681510, Dell Publishing Co., Inc.

ISBN: 0-440-11590-6

Printed in the United States of America
First U.S.A. printing—November 1982

A COFFIN
FROM THE PAST

1

The cemetery was filled with lush green weeds. They had a prim, old-fashioned look as if their forbears had been growing there for ages. But everyone knows that weeds are fast growing and must be ephemeral. This cemetery was both old and out of use. Even the newest grave in it was over a hundred years old, but everything here was civilised and well kept. The weeds were disciplined, not growing far or fast, nor trespassing much upon the graves, as if aware they had their little place in the sun and they'd better keep to it. Around the cemetery crept a square of early nineteenth-century houses, small bourgeois dwellings, flat faced and undemanding. The red brick church was a century older and had been built by Christopher Wren. Once, there had been a village here, and a village green, and the village spirit still survived, as it always does in London, even though there were now main roads and docks and factories on either side.

Coffin took his companion round the cemetery. It was a quiet spot for a walk, very nearly the only quiet one in his manor, which had a high birth rate and a high crime rate. In fact, figures for both were rising in his district to something higher than the national average. There had to be a reason for it.

'This is a short cut although it doesn't look like it,' he said cheerfully. 'We're on our way.' And then too, he had his reasons for coming here.

'I can take it slowly.'

'Yes.' I bet you can, he added to himself. It took you three days to get over from New York and you could have done it in seven hours. With still time to think things out between cups of coffee from the stewardess. Why didn't you fly out straight away?

He prodded the weeds with his foot. 'Nice old things, aren't they?' He bent down and picked a little sprigget and put it in his buttonhole. 'Had a chap in here and he said even the weeds are a species that's been extinct elsewhere in this form for a hundred years. Pharaoh's Flower, he called it.'

'I didn't imagine policemen liking weeds.'

'Oh, we're not heartless, not by any means.' And you're not long on imagination, he added. Not judging by present form. But what a beauty, he thought. And he had to admit that as well as liking weeds, he certainly liked beauties. Tall, skinny, blonde hair and covered with the most extraordinary make-up. Eyes were wearing blue and silver rings round them this year.

'The Church Commissioners wanted to tidy the graves away and use the site for something else. Perhaps sell it. Ground's valuable round here. But we persuaded them we needed it as it was. It serves a purpose in a district like this.'

'What purpose?'

Coffin looked sly. As sly, that is, as a good person can look. Until recently he hadn't thought of himself as good, indeed perhaps he hadn't been, but the quality was creeping up on him. Not good in this man's terms or that one's, but, after all, every man has his own goodness. A hard uncomfortable quality it seemed, not likely to cause him to be particularly lovable. 'It makes him very difficult to live with,' said his wife; she was not good herself. 'People come here,' he said. 'Lovers, thieves, con men. Even the odd ghost or two. It's a rendezvous. I watch it. I have people here, too. I come myself.'

'I don't believe in ghosts.'

Coffin shrugged. 'The ghosts I'm thinking of aren't always dead, poor things. One or two look as if they are. No, ghosts are people who are living on something other than oxygen and bread and water like you and me, on other things.'

The woman pulled her coat closer in the chill spring wind. She had on a smart pale coat that must have looked gay as it stepped on board the jet at John F. Kennedy Airport, but which looked almost too delicate in South London. She wasn't in mourning, anyway.

'It looks too quiet to be important,' she said.

'Naturally it's quiet. Things get fixed up where there aren't people. We *need* this place. So when we laid it on the line they let us keep it.'

'Do you come here much?'

'Not in person, no. The sight of me is apt to clear other visitors out.' In the last few years, as he had got thinner, greyer, he had begun to look formidable. There was a little thread of scar on his forehead where a blow had nearly killed him. I did die really, he had said once, the person who came back wasn't the same as the one who went down. 'This is our path through the graves to the gate.' He indicated the way.

The beautiful grey eyes looked where he pointed and looked away again. They remained calm. She nodded slightly as if telling him to go ahead.

And you don't look heartbroken, desolate, lost, my girl, he thought. You have yourself well in control. I like that in a woman, but it bears watching.

'What other things do they live on, your ghosts?' she said thoughtfully, picking her way delicately through the grass and weeds. On her feet were pale glossy shoes pretending expensively to be baby crocodile.

'Drugs, drink, methylated spirits. And one or two just live on other people,' he said. 'I think they take a little drink of some relation's blood for breakfast and come back for a nibble for tea. They look quite nice and human those people, but look closer and you'll see. Look at their relations. They give the game away; they look dried out.'

'I know one or two people like that.'

'Don't we all? You can be one yourself without knowing.' And perhaps you are, he added to himself. Camilla, the fair vampire. Ash-blonde hair, pale lips, cold eyes and a beauty, it all fitted.

She received this silently and walked on ahead. Following, he observed that the coat was cashmere and that something finer and silkier was mixed with it; and the shoes,

he now saw, were in fact made from the smallest and most
delicate of alligators. An albino one, judging from the
colour. I suppose that's what's known as being well heeled,
he thought. Money she'd earned herself, no doubt. Nothing
in the evidence he knew suggested that much money was
flowing her way from anyone else.

Across the road from the cemetery he could see the sun
shining on the windows of the Museum of London History.
Probably it was the smallest dustiest museum in the whole
of London, too. The dust, made up as it must be of years
and years of London life, dried down and powdered, was
part of the history. A living history, because the dust was
certainly added to daily. Coffin acknowledged it, but every
time he went in there, which was often lately, it made him
sneeze. He sneezed now.

"That's the Museum, isn't it?' she said, looking round.

'Yes. You lived near by for a time, didn't you?'

'Yes.' Without adding more, she turned and walked on.

She knew the district well enough, then, without being
intimate with it. However, it would be difficult for so
striking a figure to move around in it without being noticed.

'Till you went to New York?'

'Yes, till then.' She still had no more to add. No talker,
this one.

'How did you find it?'

'I enjoyed it.'

Yes, you can enjoy it, in a way, if you just live here,
thought Coffin. If you live and work here as a policeman,
then you are bound to see it with different eyes. He had
been born nearby and was truly a local. In those circumstances, while appreciating the vitality and cheerfulness of
the district, you also knew that it had more than its share
of criminals, some of them dangerous. On the other hand,
it had a lower percentage of unmarried mothers; the usual
number of drug takers; a few more psychopaths than he
probably knew about. He saw the pattern of its life in his
mind as a sort of catherine wheel, with the mass of ordinary
citizens making up the solid centre and the rest spiralling
off from it. That bright, red spark was a murderer.

'Not far from Westminster is it?'

'Not far. Too far for the Division Bell.' The Division Bell rings in the House of Commons when a vote has to be taken. There is a useful device by which those M.P.s who live near enough can have a bell synchronised to the Division Bell in their own house. And then those lucky men run round and burst, panting presumably, into the right lobby.

'It rings when M.P.s have got to vote?'

'A Division, they call it a Division, they divide the House.' She spoke with boredom, as if the whole apparatus of political life was soured for her. 'They divide it into two parts. They *pretend* there are only two parties, there are dozens really, all trying to scramble to the surface.' She knew it all, even to the number of unborn parties.

They were passing a flat slab of grey stone with deeply incised lettering. The light caught it, and the inscription stood out.

BENEATH THIS STONE LIE
THE MORTAL REMAINS OF ESTHER STEINBERG,
WIFE OF ISAIAH STEINBERG, SILVERWORKER,
AND OF REBECCA, AGED FOURTEEN YEARS,
AND JAEL, AGED TWELVE YEARS,
THEIR DAUGHTERS
ALSO OF
DAVID AGED SEVENTEEN THEIR SON.
ALSO OF
ADAH STEINBERG MOTHER OF THE ABOVE
ISAIAH
AND WIDOW OF DAVID STEINBERG LATE
OF DRESDEN
ALL MURDERED BY THE HAND OF THE SAID
ISAIAH STEINBERG ON THE FOURTEENTH OF MAY 1820.
THE SOULS OF THE RIGHTEOUS ARE IN THE HAND OF GOD.

He knelt down.

The woman saw it and stared down at it. 'He killed the lot, everyone. His mother, his wife and all his children.'

A pale glove slipped from her hand and dropped on the stone. Coffin bent to pick it up. 'Well, that's family life for you,' he said.

The pale grey eyes stared at him calmly, assessing what he said. Or so he thought. You can never be quite sure with people. Perhaps she was all broken up inside.

'You mean there's a better chance of being murdered by someone within the family circle than outside it?'

'There's always a relationship. And the family relationship is sharpest and closest and most easily heated up.'

'That won't be much use to you in the present case, will it? There's no family.'

'At the moment it looks totally inexplicable.' He added: 'But that doesn't mean there isn't an explanation.'

'Or that it won't be uncovered?'

'In the end.'

'For someone in public life, as he was, I suppose there could always be a public motive? Assassination, I suppose I mean.'

'I'm sorry, but in this case there are things that suggest it wasn't so here.'

She was silent.

The big iron gate moved easily as he opened it. There was a lock, as old by its look as the cemetery itself; but no one ever used it, this place was never locked and the key was long since lost. In the corner by the gate was a wire rubbish bin.

'Does this place mean anything to you? Any special associations?'

'No, I was never here before.'

'But you lived near. You must have seen it.'

'I lived here for about eight weeks nearly two years ago. I was just married. I didn't notice it.'

'Neither of you?'

'How can I answer that?' She turned back to look at the small enclosed area of antique graves. 'Was someone here then? The night,' she hesitated, 'the night when it happened?'

For answer he pointed to the waste bin. 'In that bin are three pieces of toffee paper and a paper bag. I can see them. Not much. All put there by children, I dare say. If we checked we'd find they were all very local children, living in the nearest streets. Because you can't see this bin. It's not very obvious. You have to know it's there.'

He put his hand in the bin and drew out the bits of paper. Two pieces had held chocolate toffees, and the third small piece some butterscotch. The paper bag had held fish and chips and had the name of the street on it. Czar Peter Street, just round the corner from where they stood. Silently he put them back.

'We found a paper mask in that basket three mornings ago. A paper mask roughly cut out of white paper. There was a smear of blood right across one corner.'

She absorbed this without comment. Then, 'That means something?'

'Well, it could.'

The gate closed behind them. They crossed the street. This terrace of houses was Hanover Row. Round the corner lay Great Barnabas Street. Half way down the street was a house with a policeman outside it.

'This is the house," said Coffin quietly.

Camilla looked up quietly, studying it. 'I was never here. This set up didn't exist when I went away. Tom had another office.'

'No.' Coffin was watching her. 'It's been going about twelve months. But you had the address?'

'Oh yes.' She turned away. 'Tell me. Tell me now. No one has yet. Now you do it.'

'It was on the ground floor. There are three steps up to the front door with all these houses, as you see, then the front door opens straight into a front room with a door in the inner wall leading into another room. This isn't the case with the other houses in this street. The others open into a little hall with two rooms, one front and one back, leading off. They were only little working men's cottages when they were built. This house, No. 12, was specially altered.'

'I know about that. He wrote.'

'The girl's body was found lying in the front room as if she'd come hurrying forward. Mr. Barr was just behind.

She must have been shot first, but she wasn't dead when she was found. She managed to say a few words before she died.'

'I see.' Camilla was white. 'Go on.'

'It looked as though they must have been . . .' he hesitated, 'together in the inner room and she heard a noise in the outer room and went through.'

'Still go on,' said Camilla. 'There is something more, isn't there?'

He hesitated.

'Remember I have some right to know all this.'

'She, the girl, wasn't wearing very much.'

'And my husband?' said Camilla harshly. 'After all, he *was* my husband.'

'Just trousers,' said Coffin.

On the evening of June 6 Thomas Barr, M.P. and his secretary had been at work in the house in Great Barnabas Street. They were working in the small inner room which had a glass panel in the upper part of the door. It was clouded glass so that you couldn't see out or in, but you could certainly see if the light was on and someone was working in there. The outer door to the street was always left unlocked on Friday evenings and callers let themselves into the waiting room. Friday night was surgery night. All M.P.s have what they call their surgery, when they see men and women from their constituencies who have problems and want help. It's like a doctor's surgery. Some patients come in with genuine complaints and deeply need help, others are not really sick, but needing someone to talk to, and just a few are the neurotic and maladjusted who always have a grievance and can never be satisfied. Occasionally you get the violent calls. One M.P. had to defend himself from an acid attack and another, in the North of England, had his surgery burnt down. Everyone gets mad letters and these are usually ignored.

The police keep a special eye on all M.P.s because they know they are a focus for certain sorts of trouble. Coffin watched Great Barnabas Street and Tom Barr in an unobtrusive way. Things seemed to go quietly there; he never had any trouble.

Until three days ago. Three days ago someone, so far unknown, had come to the door of No. 12 Great Barnabas Street, pushed it open and gone inside. He, or she, must have made some sort of noise, perhaps even shouted or called, because the girl had come out of the inner room. He may, or may not, have been wearing a mask. The girl's body had been found near the outer door; the man was lying across the threshold of the inner room. So it looked as though the girl had come running out and the man had followed.

They had been found by Clement Grove, one of Barr's panel of volunteer workers, who often visited the surgery on Friday evening for a talk, and to see if his help was needed. This night it was.

'Yes, I remember Clem,' said Camilla, her voice sounding far away, as if prompted by a distant memory. 'Yes, I do remember Clem. The one with the birthmark.'

'He's got rid of that now.'

'He helped when Tom was fighting the seat. He was there on Election Night. He always seemed so inarticulate.'

'He's learnt a few words since then.'

'And he had some kind of speech defect. More a sort of slowness than anything else. I suppose he was just sensitive really.'

'That's been getting treatment.'

'He was working in the Museum. Curator? Assistant Curator?'

'He's a Curator now.'

'So it was he who found them,' said Camilla. 'All the time I was travelling over I wondered about that, trying to imagine who it could have been, what it must have felt like. I never thought of Clem. I was fond of Clem.'

'He was a regular Friday evening visitor. Had been these last few months.'

'And so he walked in on them? It must have been a big shock. Especially . . . the way it was. As I remember, Clem was quite shy. He'd mind finding them the way they were more than them being dead.'

Coffin shook his head.

'Perhaps he knew, though. Perhaps someone told him. That sort of thing gets out, you know. Of course you know. Perhaps someone said: drop in without knocking one Friday evening and guess what you'll see.'

'Don't do it to yourself.'

'And did he describe the scene? How did he describe it to you? I bet he couldn't find words to put it into, in spite of all his speech training lessons. Nor you either. You've been carefully fumbling that ball, haven't you? But I could find words.'

Coffin was silent.

'How I hate your damn mealy-mouthedness,' cried Camilla.

And you don't act exactly like a broken-hearted widow, thought Coffin.

2

On that evening, now three days ago, Thomas Barr and his secretary Sheila were together in the inner office of the house in Great Barnabas Street. Surgery time. He was on the telephone. He was a tall man, as fair as his wife, but whereas she had pale grey eyes, his were brown. She was fine boned and he was sturdy. Although they were so much alike, you would never have mistaken them for brother and sister. He had her photograph on his desk. Constituents liked to see their M.P.'s wife's photographs about, it gave them that safe family feeling. If there were children, their photograph should be displayed too, preferably with their mother or an animal, it didn't really matter which, both were British. If neither was available, then the children with a bicycle would do, one bicycle between them, not one each, which would hint at extravagance. (No M.P. can be extravagant.) There is something very reassuring about a bicycle. In this case there was no bicycle, no animal, no mother, no children. But there was a charming photograph of Camilla. Unluckily she looked extremely expensive. Tom could be expensive too when he liked. He had as much a taste for elegant, well-designed objects as she had. Perhaps that was why he had married Camilla. Outside the house now stood a graceful foreign motor car. Inside his office the filing cabinets were bright and new, the typewriter a clear red. On account of it, Sheila used no nail enamel.

Thomas put the receiver down. The telephone promptly rang again. This time, with a rueful smile at him, Sheila answered it. 'Really not too many waiting for you tonight,' she said. 'A few appointments. And I suppose Fred will be in.'

Fred Dick was Tom's political agent. They met regularly.

'He's coming to see me on Saturday,' said Tom. 'It's his wife's birthday.'

'Then it's going to be a quiet night,' said Sheila.

It was seven-thirty. There were to be six more telephone calls between now and nine, after which time no one answered the telephone bell.

Sheila could deal with this call herself and she did. 'South Oulton Co-operative Society wanting you to make the winding up speech at their Weekend School on Disarmament.' By the people who ask him to address them, so shall you know an M.P.'s politics. Also, his standing in the world. But Tom Barr's rating was rising. They both knew it. He had served his time on committees, he had worked diligently as a Parliamentary Private Secretary, he had travelled to Vietnam and Biafra. He was next in the line for promotion and the newspapers had been hinting it would come soon.

'I'll go if the dates work.'

'That's what I said. They're going to write.'

'I needn't stay the night. I can drive over and drive back.'

Sheila got up and moved away from the table. 'I'll make some coffee.'

They drank some coffee and worked on afterwards. He was dictating notes for a clutch of speeches in the coming week.

'This is going to be good,' said Sheila, looking up from her notes. 'You ought to get a big clap at the end of this one.'

'I'm saying what they want me to say.'

'But it's true what you say. You always come across absolutely sincere.'

'Oh yes, it's true. I don't know that I've ever said anything deliberately untrue. That would be naïve. There's no need. I just leave out what I don't choose to say. Making a

sincere speech depends on your skill in doing it. I'm quite
skilful. I've learned how to handle honesty.'

They were interrupted by a knock at the door. 'Oh that's
your eight o'clock appointment.' She looked at her engagement pad. 'Herbert Peters. Bus driver. He's anxious about
the lease of his house. Thinks he may be evicted. He's a
friend of Waldon Sweden who helped you in your cam-
paign and who recommended him to see you. Will you see
him in here or outside?'

'In here. Where's the house?'

'Poland Street, it's not far from here.'

'Yes, I know where that is. Not far from the Prince
Regent Music Hall.'

'Well, it's a repertory theatre now and you helped raise
the money to make it one, remember?'

'That's right.'

Mr. Peters was a fluent, nervous man who seemed to have
fallen into the hands of a sharp property dealer and wanted
sorting out. It wasn't Thomas's job to sort him out, but
he could let him talk, tell him where to go for advice and
promise to write a letter to back him up. Mr. Peters
departed, still talking but much more cheerful.

'You did a good job on him,' said Sheila, closing the door
behind Mr. Peters. Just occasionally she allowed herself to
walk over the bounds between a personal and a business
relationship.

The next visitor was a Trade Union official from the
docks. He came in a semi-private capacity, not wanting to
involve his Union too much, but wanting to sound out
the M.P. about some legislation he'd got wind of. He'd
heard there were some new hygiene regulations being
drafted about the docks and the handling of frozen meat
and he was unhappy about the stringency of them. He both
wanted to sound out Thomas and at the same time enlist
him in a lobby.

'I agree the hygiene needs tightening up,' he said, 'but
if these overalls and gloves are what they sound like the
men won't wear them, and if they won't wear them then
we're in trouble.'

'You seem to know more than I do about it,' said Thomas Barr. 'And you certainly know more about what your members will or will not wear.'

'Hygiene has to be looked at, I grant you that. I'm for it, but it's froth on the glass asking men to wear gloves and special uniform when you're also asking them to walk a quarter of a mile to wash their hands. You know there's only one small block of washrooms and lavatories in that area.'

Tom nodded. 'Aren't they building more?'

'Yes, but even that is only scratching at the problem. I tell you there's a need to re-think the whole problem of facilities. We had a study group on it . . .'

Thomas closed his eyes. Study groups, think-ins, he knew where it went from here.

When he opened his eyes, Jim Stubbs had gone. 'Did I go to sleep?' he asked guiltily.

'If you did, he didn't notice. You said yes and no and goodbye at the right times.'

'In my sleep probably. I did drop off. We had a late night session last night and a three-line whip.'

In the lingo of the House of Commons this meant that Members had to be there to vote or else face Party discipline. Only important issues got a three-line whip.

'I'm going away for the weekend tomorrow,' said Sheila suddenly.

'Are you?' He sounded surprised.

'It's my free Saturday and Sunday. You don't want me?'

'No, of course I don't want you.' He knew that his secretary had another part-time job, that she worked in a local hospital three weekends out of four. But she didn't usually tell him what she was doing with her spare time. Their hours together were between ten and five on all week days except Friday, when she worked late. Outside of that her life was private. 'I hope you enjoy it. You deserve a break.'

'Oh, it's not quite a holiday.' She bent her head over her work.

'It's hot in here.' Thomas took his coat off and hung it

over the back of his chair. 'Anyone else out there waiting to see me?' He nodded towards the outer room.

'No, it's empty. I just looked.'

'Quiet tonight. Is that good or bad? I'd call it good.'

'It's good,' said Sheila. She laughed.

Then followed three business calls on the telephone, which they dealt with briskly. These interrupted them a little, but not much.

It was hot in this small inner room which had one window facing on the back yard. They had this window open. As dusk came, the lights were put on and insects blundered in, attracted by the light.

At one point Sheila went and got herself a drink of water. She left the nearly full glass on the desk.

The telephone rang once more. Thomas answered it himself. He was slow getting to the telephone, finishing a sentence he was dictating to Sheila first. 'Yes,' he said. 'Who is that?' And then when he got no reply: 'Who is that?' Finally he banged the receiver down. 'Some lunatic,' he said. 'Just a lot of breathing.'

'I hate that,' said Sheila. 'I hate it when it's like that.'

'It happens,' said Thomas with a shrug. 'You're meant to hate it.'

They worked on for a few minutes, then Thomas said, 'I thought you said there was no one outside.'

She smiled at him. 'There wasn't.'

'There's someone now. Someone's come in.'

An insect was buzzing round the centre light. Sheila moved towards the window to close it against the entrance of any more. There was a line of sweat on her face.

The front door banged and then opened again shortly afterwards. They both heard it. Sheila moved towards the inner door. She looked back at Thomas who gave her a smile as earlier she had smiled at him. Between a smile and a smile sometimes a gulf opens.

3

Coffin held open the front door of No. 12 Great Barnabas
Street for Camilla Barr to walk ahead. He nodded to the
single policeman on guard in the street.

That morning the papers had been hinting that behind
the death of Thomas Barr lay scandal and depravity. The
imagination of everyone was titillated by the macabre
death scene, and because the police had released so few
details, salacious inventions were rampant. The European
press had already picked up the story, as had the American, and was reporting it in a rapt reproving way. English
political scandals always had an especial appeal.

Camilla had regained her control after her outburst.
Very possibly she had benefited from it. Coffin felt something had eased inside her. He hesitated, wanting to make
what must be a bad moment as easy as possible for her.
But she took it well, observing the room and not flinching.

'Yes, these are Tom's things. He wrote and asked my
advice even after I was in New York.' She looked around
and gave a mirthless laugh. 'I don't think he took it. So
this is where it happened?'

She didn't wait for an answer but moved into the middle
of the room and stood looking. The room was small, the
walls painted a shiny cream, the floor carpeted in a dun-
coloured haircord. There was a picture of Clement Attlee
on the wall and upright chairs lined the walls. In the
centre of the room was a table with old magazines on it.
Camilla knew they were old magazines because they always
had been. Except for the photograph on the wall it could
have been a dentist's or a doctor's waiting room.

'Most M.P.s have a photograph of themselves on the

wall, Thomas has a Prime Minister,' observed Camilla in a detached way. 'That tells you something about him.'

It tells me something about you, too, thought Coffin: you are right outside the stream of your husband's life. You may have loved him or you may not, I'll wait to make up my mind on that one, but your ambitions and his were not identified.

Silently Camilla went to the door of the inner room, opened it and stood there quietly studying the room where her husband had spent the last hours of his life. No one was quite sure yet of exactly what had happened in those hours.

In this house there were only two floors and a small basement. The basement was derelict, not used, all entrances to it blocked. The top floor was let out to a club which had been formed to study U.F.O. sightings, but after holding a few meetings there the club had gone out of existence and was trying to sell the lease. A locked door at the top of the staircase separated the two floors.

In this confined area on the ground floor, with a front window overlooking the road, two people had died violently. The room had witnessed the violence and its walls had contained and given shelter to the scene. Now it lay quiet and undisturbed, yet not without speech to tell what it knew.

But you have to know how to interpret this speech. Coffin had learnt. No violent act can be performed in a room without leaving silent traces. A chair displaced, a glass which had contained water knocked over, papers scattered from a table. A smear of blood on the dun-coloured carpet.

'It's stuffy in here,' said Camilla.

Coffin nodded. 'We've had it locked up.'

'I used to provide flowers for the office,' said Camilla. 'I see he'd given that up.' She ran a finger along the edge of the table. 'Quite clean, really. I suppose the secretary saw to that?'

'I believe she did.'

'I didn't know her, you know. No, we'd never met.' Camilla walked away to look into Attlee's face. 'So there wasn't that between us. Whatever there was. And who knows?'

'Nice girl.'

'Was she married?'

'Widow.'

'Accident or natural causes? Or murder, like me?' said Camilla in a hard, bright tone.

'I'm afraid I don't know how her husband died,' said Coffin, who did not wish to discuss it.

'Don't you think you ought to find out?'

The room still smelt of cigarette smoke. Someone had dragged a chair up to the inner door and sat just to one side of it, smoking and dropping butts into a saucer. The cigarettes had been removed, and the saucer, but a burn in the carpet showed where a butt had fallen wide of the saucer.

Absently Camilla straightened the chair, placing it against the wall, and then went into the inner room and looked at her husband's desk. 'So you tidied things up?'

'We had to a bit, but the desk still looks much as it did.'

'Then the secretary was tidy. Tom didn't naturally keep his desk this way. But he was a hard worker.' For the first time her voice softened. 'He worked as hard as anyone I've ever known.' She looked at Coffin. 'You look as though you're a hard worker.'

She stood for a little while by the desk. Her own photograph was on the desk and she picked it up. 'I had that done when we got married. It was for Tom, but somehow he never liked it.' She put the photograph down. 'It was the place I couldn't stand, you know, not Tom. The place and the life we had to live. So I went away. I suppose I thought in the end he'd follow me, but he went right on living the life he'd always led.' She looked at Coffin. 'Until now,' she said.

She had a disquieting way of putting a flag on a fact and waving it at you. Coffin could see she hadn't been an ideal M.P.'s wife.

She looked at her watch. 'I believe I've seen enough of this room.' Delicately she skirted a glass which still lay on the floor.

'Had they been . . .' She hesitated. 'Drinking? Had they been drinking?'

Coffin shook his head. 'The glass had contained water. But it was empty.' Not spilt on the floor. As far as they could see it had been emptied or drunk. A few drops had remained when they picked it up and looked. Then they put it back and photographed it.

'And so, they were in here . . . doing whatever they were doing . . . when someone came in the door and shot them. The girl got shot first and then my husband.'

'That's the way it seems.'

'Wasn't the door locked?'

'Not that night.'

'No, Friday night it stayed open. I remember that.' She shook her head. 'You'd think they'd have locked the door, wouldn't you? It was rash. But sometimes I think people have a built-in desire to destroy themselves. They set up the situation for it. Perhaps Thomas was such a one.'

Thomas Barr had had his desk with the telephone on it by the window in the back room and Sheila had had a table in front of the other window. On Sheila's table was a big ink stain as if she had knocked over a bottle of ink. It was a fresh stain.

'Did your husband have normal health?' asked Coffin suddenly.

Camilla was surprised. 'I think so. Yes, he was a perfectly healthy man. Who's normal? But he was healthy.'

The chair behind Tom Barr's desk was padded and covered with a light tweed. A square of cloth had been gouged from the right side.

The police had gone over the room with great care. Amongst other things they looked for blood on the chair. There was none. But they discovered a heavy concentration of the minerals and salts deposited by the body in perspiration. Whoever had sat in that chair had sweated heavily. Sweat, like blood, answers to various identification tests. The blood groups A and B can be identified in sweat except for that of an interesting minority who are non-secretors. The person who had sat in this chair and sweated had been of blood group A. Thomas Barr had also been of blood group A. The presumption was that it was his sweat.

Camilla saw Coffin's eyes rest on the chair. 'I chose that chair. Got it covered specially. All by remote control in New York.'

'There's a lot of sweat on it. Some illnesses have that symptom. I wondered.'

'I don't know if Tom was ill. I don't think so. Perhaps he just had plenty to sweat about. I reckon he did, poor Tom.' She turned her own photograph face down on the desk. 'He must have hated me watching him, and I don't really know why I did. Not any longer. You should never watch anyone when you're not there.' She laughed. 'You get to see some unexpected things.'

Coffin observed her. He had been observing her all the time. Everyone took shock differently, of course. Maybe this was her way. But the question you could ask yourself about her was: what was the nature of the shock and when was it received?

Camilla turned away from the inner room (which was trying to shout out its story) and walked towards the front door. 'At least it was quick for them,' she said.

A flight from New York is quick too. No one had been notified of her arrival and no one had met her. She looked the sort of girl who knew how to arrange things. Suppose she'd already been over here and stood outside this house in Great Barnabas Street and then come inside? It could be she was not weeping now because the tears had already been wept.

'It wasn't so quick for the girl,' said Coffin. 'She was half conscious. Perhaps she had been lying there for quite a time.'

'Oh.' Camilla considered. 'Can't you tell?'

'There was a time of thirty minutes when no telephone calls were answered. They were discovered at 9.30. Between 9 and 9.30 is what we call a 'dead time.' We don't know, can't pinpoint when within this period the attack happened.'

'And the girl didn't say anything?'

'She just had time to say two words.'

He paused, then went on. 'She said: Charlie Grinling. That's all.'

'Oh well,' began Camilla.

'Only we don't have the least idea in the world who Charlie Grinling was and why he should have killed her.'

All around them noises of a house that has been lived in for over a hundred years were repeating themselves as they had done through the years. The floor boards where their feet had pressed moved slowly back into position with gentle creaks, plaster pattered down in the wall cavity with a sound like little feet, and a door banged. It was a restless house.

'Where did that door bang?' said Camilla suddenly.

'Upstairs.'

'I thought the house was empty.'

'The Club which rented the rooms there is moving out.'

'I hate the sounds of footsteps in an empty house,' said Camilla. She shivered.

The sounds increased, someone was up there dragging something heavy across the floor.

'What are they doing?' asked Camilla.

'They don't have much furniture up there.' Coffin also was listening. 'I think that's bundles of newspapers they are dragging across the floor. Mostly it's newspapers they have. Naturally, they're always looking for reports.'

'What sort of a club are they, then?'

'A sort of scientific club. They're watching. Watching for visitors from space. Flying saucers, green men, that sort of thing. But they're folding up. They've had various crises and the members have left.'

'Then who's that up there?'

'A nice old girl called Miss Jones. The newspapers were her property. She came just now and asked me if she could take the stuff.'

Footsteps sounded on the stairs and the door on the stairs opened and an elderly woman appeared. She was wearing a head scarf and a flowered apron. She looked more than a little frail, but very alert. She managed to look very much in charge, as if this was a school and she was the headmistress.

'Did you call?' she said.

'No.'

'I'm just off.' She took off her apron, rolling it up and putting it under her arm. 'The job's done. You'll get some-one to bring the papers round to me, Superintendent? I can't carry things since my operation.'

'I will.' They seemed on good terms, the policeman and the elderly gentlewoman. She smiled and gave a silent bow to Camilla, but did not speak to her. Almost certainly she knew who Camilla was. 'I'm glad to be going really. This place would never have done for us. The emanations are not right.'

'What emanations?' asked Camilla.

'One thing after another,' murmured Miss Jones. 'One cannot overlook it. A continuous string of violence.'

'How I hate it when you mumble and eye each other and don't look at me,' cried Camilla. 'Tell me what you mean!'

Far away in New York she had had a bright new flat high up on the fourteenth floor. Everything in it had been seemly and quiet and clean, nothing touched it. Down in the street things raged and roared, but up where Camilla lived was gentle living. Plastic wrapped, Camilla had felt safe. Camilla incommunicada. And this was what she wanted. 'What sort of a house is this?' cried Camilla.

Miss Jones said: 'Isaiah Steinberg killed his whole family in this house in 1820, three years after it was built. Then in 1890 a girl was strangled here. And now . . . your husband, dear. I recognised you. I saw you on Election Night. I voted for your husband. He should never have taken this house. Whose idea was it?'

'It was empty, Tom said, and going cheap.'

'This house is never empty,' Miss Jones said. 'And the price it asked isn't cheap.'

'That sort of talk is rubbish.'

'You should never have left him alone.'

And you should never let people like Miss Jones go on talking, thought Coffin, not only will they say anything but they will also say the truth.

'Lock that door, won't you?' he asked. Miss Jones went

to the door which separated the two floors and turned the key. Coffin watched. 'And I'll have the key. It's the only one?' She nodded. 'And you have one to the front door? Right, I'll have that too.'

The three of them left the house together, Coffin pocketing all the keys.

'Do you have any keys to this house?' he asked Camilla.

She hesitated and then said: 'Yes, as a matter of fact I do.' Unobtrusively she looked at her watch. Coffin, who had excellent eyesight, could see that she hadn't adjusted it properly to the transatlantic time change and it was an hour slow. 'I collected them from my husband's party agent.'

'May I have them, please?'

'Is it really necessary?'

'You'll get them back.'

She looked in her bag and after fumbling a little withdrew a key ring with two keys which were newly cut. But wives do have keys to their husband's property.

Coffin took them.

'Oh, you've got gloves on,' said Miss Jones brightly. 'It's ages since I've seen a man in gloves. Or are your hands cold?'

'Yes, very,' said Coffin. 'It's a sort of complaint that policemen suffer from.'

Camilla looked at the keys and the gloves; she was puzzled. But she was moving into strange country where appearances were deceptive and nothing was quite what it seemed.

'Well, you've seen it all now,' said Coffin, when they got outside. There was a black police car at the kerb. 'Do you want to be driven anywhere?'

'No. My husband's private apartment is near here. I still have the key.'

'I can still drive you.' He was watching her. 'If you're in a hurry.'

'No, no, no hurry,' she said, gathering her pale sophisticated coat around her. 'I feel a little sick. A walk on my own would do me good.'

'We shall have to talk again,' said Coffin.

'Yes. I know.' She was serious. 'I'll always be ready.' She raised her hand in farewell.

'You can't be alone there, my dear,' said Miss Jones.

'I shan't be. My little cousin Jen's going to be there.'

Miss Jones watched her go. 'I think she must be going to meet someone, don't you?' she said.

'And she's late for it,' said Coffin. 'One hour late.'

As he and Miss Jones parted, she put her hand on Coffin's arm and said earnestly: 'Take care of yourself. I have a dear friend who is a seer and she told me she sees a policeman falling. It could be you.'

Coffin half heard her words; he absorbed them into his mind, but most of his attention was directed towards Camilla's retreating back.

Camilla murmured to herself as she ran. 'I know what I'll do. I'll call out "Jen, Jen, dear, is that you?"'

It would not be Jen and she knew it; but the words might protect her.

4

The dreams men dream when they are on their own are not invariably masculine in quality, sometimes a feminine element creeps in. Coffin, sitting in his new office, in the very new police station recently erected almost opposite the old one, was thinking that the smell of new paint was sickening and the heaps of sawdust and plaster that still seemed to appear magically in the corners of rooms were depressing. 'If I had a dust pan and brush I'd get up and shift it,' he thought, looking at a pile near the window which had, he thought, been there for a week. But although this new block of offices had everything, had central heating and air conditioning and new sorts of telephones that made a fluting noise, it did not have a brush and pan. Cleaning was done by huge machines that hummed and sucked. Only sometimes, as in his room, they seemed to spit out, too. He was dreaming of order, cleanliness and perpetual quiet.

They had rising crime figures in this district. You had to remember that, when they were falling elsewhere. There must be a reason for it. Coffin blamed it on the new building; the old one had been better. 'A man's only as good as his building,' he muttered to himself.

He left his own room and walked down two flights of highly polished stairs to a room on the ground floor made over to be the headquarters of the investigation into the death of Thomas Barr, M.P. Earlier this day there had been a press conference here.

William Dove, Coffin's subordinate, was moodily turning over some papers. 'You walked down,' he said.

'Yes.'

'I can hear your breathing. You need more exercise.'

'There's something wrong with that lift.' He didn't say anything of Miss Jones's warning.

'Yes, I know. It stuck this morning with the Assistant Commissioner, Plain Clothes Branch, inside it and stayed there for half an hour.'

'He didn't fall?'

'No. Did you want him to?'

'I just wondered. We got any seers in the district?'

'Any what?'

'Seers. People who look into the future. A friend of Miss Jones.'

Dove considered. 'I heard Plowman's back. If there's anything like that in the district it usually starts with him and his wife. And they certainly know Miss Jones. They were all in that club together before Plowman blew.'

'So he's back.'

'Yes, a few weeks ago. His wife never left, of course. Been here all the time. I don't know what he's taken up now. But there'll be something. He's never without an interest.'

'Is Miss Jones sane?'

'Jonesy's all right. She just sees things other people don't.'

'She upset Mrs. Barr. Me too, a bit. That house is bad enough anyway at the moment.' He looked round the room. 'Got any tea?'

Dove went to the door and shouted an order. 'The tea's worse here, too, have you noticed?' he said comfortably. 'So you ought to have shut Jonesy up. She always says things you'd rather not hear said aloud. She used to teach me scripture. That's how she got interested in Flying Saucers—from the Old Testament. And the widow's upset? Well, she's got plenty to upset her, I'd say.'

'I can't make her out,' admitted Coffin. 'She is not easy to know. But she knew more about the arrangement of the furniture in that inner room than she should have done if she'd never seen it. She put a chair back in just the right place.'

'Could be intelligent guesswork.'

'And she has keys to the house. I have the keys. I'd just like to know what fingerprints are on them and if they match any we've found in the house.' He handed them to Dove. 'I took care my prints didn't get on them. I wore gloves.'

'That'd be nice,' said Dove wistfully. 'A bit of luck like that would come in handy.'

'And we'd better make a check about when Camilla Barr did enter the country. No one met her. I'm not convinced she arrived when she said she did. She's deep. On the other hand, her watch was an hour slow, which suggests she had to alter it after flying the Atlantic and hadn't got it correct.'

'Or the watch may just be slow,' said Dove.

'Yes.' Coffin grinned. 'Whatever, she's running an hour late.'

'We can't trace any Charlie Grinling,' said Dove. 'Whatever the girl meant by the name it means nothing to us. Not a householder, not on the electoral roll. Wasn't born or died here. Didn't go to school here.'

'I never thought it would be easy to find Charlie Grinling,' said Coffin. He looked at the clock. Twelve o'clock noon. And it was still under an hour since he had left Camilla Barr.

'Jen, Jen . . .' called Camilla, as she opened the front door of her husband's flat. 'Jen, is that you?' She tried to be brave, but her voice wavered.

There was no answer.

'Oh God,' she said wearily, 'playing coy? Come on out and let me see you. I know you're here.'

Still there was nothing.

'I know you're there. I can smell. Hear that? I can smell.'

A wisp of smoke floated out from the door. He must be nearer to her than she had guessed.

'You're late,' he said.

* * *

'She's meeting someone, you know,' said Coffin. 'If she's meeting someone it's in that apartment. Have we put someone on it?'

Dove spoke. 'We went over it initially, of course. The man on duty reports on it. But there's no special watch.'

'We may have slipped there.' He frowned. But he knew it was a question of men. In this last three weeks there had been a smallish bank raid, a case of arson and a rape.

'The extra man we had detailed to us from Z went the day of the Shiner's Wharf job,' said Dove, underlining what he already knew.

But because he had been having feminine dreams, a feminine thought came to Coffin. 'Let's ring her up,' he said. 'Let's be a voice out of the blue.'

Camilla was reluctant to answer the telephone when she heard it ring.

'Probably it's Jen,' she said. 'My cousin.'

'Probably it's not,' said the man. 'Does she usually ring?'

'No.' She listened to the persistent ring. 'I won't answer it.'

'Answer it.' He guided her hand to the telephone, but gently. 'Don't you know enough to do that? Act normal. It's normal to answer the 'phone.'

Camilla answered, speaking quietly as if she hoped he couldn't hear. What she said was very little and her voice gave little away. Her shoulder was hunched instinctively, as if she wanted to shield herself from the man who was watching. She put the receiver down.

'That was the police.' Her voice was still quiet, even tranquil. 'They're suspicious.'

'Suspicious? You bet they're suspicious. They're always suspicious. It's what keeps them going. They're watching you, lady.' He added gently. 'But they didn't see anyone come in. You've got you a professional.'

'I don't want to hide anything,' said Camilla stiffly. 'My connection with you . . .' her voice faltered, 'is perfectly straightforward.'

* * *

'She's got someone there. Probably a man. Of that I'm
nearly sure.' Coffin nodded.

'You didn't hear anything?' asked Dove.

'No, he never spoke.' Coffin looked across the room and
out of the window to the South London scene. 'All the
same, he was there.'

He looked at his watch. 'I have,' he said, 'thirty minutes.
Let's go round to the house in Great Barnabas Street.'
Thirty minutes out of a day in which he had to attend a
Committee on Crime Prevention (which for him was a
black joke), attend to routine, and buy a new pair of shoes.
Buying a new pair of shoes was the height of his private
life at the moment.

'You and me? I haven't got thirty minutes,' protested
Dove.

'We'll do it in twenty five.' He had the door already
open.

'You didn't drink your tea.'

'You were right about the flavour,' said Coffin. 'It's
worse.'

Once again they were in the front room of the house in
Great Barnabas Street and once again the front door had
closed behind them with its little thump, shutting them in
with the smell of dust, and new paint and old, old life.

'On the night, that door was closed but not locked,' said
Coffin. 'People knocked and came in.'

'Someone did just that,' said Dove.

'Why is there such a smell of paint in here?' asked
Coffin irritably.

'He'd had the window frames repainted twice within
the last few weeks,' said Dove.

'Twice?'

'Perhaps they didn't do the job right the first time,' said
Dove.

'Didn't he have the inside painted as well?'

'Apparently not.'

'Who did the job?'

'Poulton's, I believe. Poulton's of Lazarus Street,' said
Dove, who always knew that sort of fact, although not

always what to make of it. He made a note. 'I'll go and
see them.'

'Yes, do that. See what they have to say. Have a look at
the bill.'

'Yes.' Dove considered. 'Why?'

'To see if they charged for it twice, of course,' said
Coffin, turning away.

Both men were standing in the outer room. To their
left was the staircase which ran up to the next floor with
the locked door at the top.

'I suppose the attacker did come in through the front
door that night and not down the staircase?'

He had asked this question not once but several times
and always the answer had come up that the door at the
top of the staircase had been locked on that night, and
was locked when the murder was discovered.

'We can't really be sure,' explained Dove patiently, once
again. 'As you know,' he added, the patience wearing a
bit thin at that point. 'But there's no sign that door was
opened that night.'

'He could have been waiting upstairs to come down and
surprise them when they were alone. And they could have
had the front door locked. Which he unlocked when he
left.'

'I don't think that would explain too much,' said Dove.

'It would explain *them*,' said Coffin. 'Otherwise I don't
understand them, do you?'

Their eyes met. Behind each man's eyes lay the image of
two people, a girl and a man who had bled to death on
this floor.

'Folks,' said Dove with a shrug. He used this as an
abbreviation. There's nowt so queer as folks was a favourite
remark of his and one he used often. Whenever he couldn't
understand human behaviour, and this happened often
lately, he said 'Folks'. It meant that he had switched off.

'She had on a thin white silk slip. Nothing else. He had
on grey trousers. Again, nothing else. I don't get it.'

'Don't you?' said Dove sardonically. The psychology of
events might be beyond him, but the actual events them-

selves he thought he could see plain enough. He attempted a little imagination. 'There are people like that. A sort of Russian roulette, you know.'

'He was M.P. for this constituency, this was one of his working nights.'

'Might have given a bit more taste to it,' said Dove. He was a stolid man himself, not easily moved, and was all for things having a high flavour. He liked pickles.

'You're making them out maniacs,' said Coffin. 'There's the girl too, remember. Was she playing Russian roulette too?'

'Well, you need two for that sort,' said Dove, unmoved, even by the picture he was drawing.

'He was a steady hardworking man, ambitious, anxious. He cared about the people here, and he minded about his career.'

'But his wife had left him a year ago,' said Dove. 'More than that.'

'But the girl was . . .' he paused.

'And she was a widow,' said Dove.

'Yes,' said Coffin. 'Maybe that's the right way to end that sentence.'

He walked over to the front door. A short distance in, a white chalk circle was drawn on the floor as if marking it.

He put his foot on it. One pace in.

'And that was where we found the lump of earth?'

'It was.'

'Who put the chalk mark there?'

'A new lad called Perkins.'

'He's got a sense of humour.'

'No, he's dead earnest. He's still taking his training seriously, they said at Detective School. So he is marking everything.'

Coffin put his foot on the spot again. 'It must have dropped off the attacker's foot as he put it inside the door.'

'Looks like it.'

Coffin sat down on the chair which Camilla had moved and cupped his left hand as if he held in it that little piece of earth. 'And in that piece of mud was a leaf of a weed.

Pharaoh's weed grown in the old burying place. And so we searched. And in the rubbish bin was a paper mask, with a stain on it.'

'Origin unknown,' said Dove.

'Of course. Might mean nothing. Might mean everything.' He went to the window and looked out on the calm and empty South London street. 'In God's name, what did happen in this room on that night?'

On that night, Thomas Barr and his secretary found the heat trying. The hot spell had arrived unexpectedly. For days previously it had been raining and raining. The soil in the old graveyard was soaked, and then the sun came out and the temperature went up.

It was still and quiet in the room where they worked; distantly a few outside sounds of traffic drifted in.

Tom raised his head and listened. 'It's one of those minutes that seem to go on and on, isn't it? As if time had come to a stop.'

Sheila smiled. 'I know what you mean: when it's hot, and still, with just a little noise from somewhere far away. When I was little I used to think these are the minutes I shall remember when I'm old. But it isn't true. I have forgotten them. They've all floated away.'

'They may still be going on somewhere,' said Tom, half seriously, half mockingly. 'And you may still be remembering.'

'That would be a sort of hell, wouldn't it?' said Sheila, 'to be stuck in one moment for ever and ever.' In spite of the heat, she shivered. 'What a horrible way of being a ghost.'

Many traditions believe time is a cycle. The followers of the Vedanta believe that the spirit must work its way through many lives before it can escape to non-existence. The spirits of those who die by violence have a particular check to these movement of their souls, and may be fixed for aeons at the moment of their violent dissolution.

'I'm going away for the weekend,' said Sheila suddenly.

'Are you?' He sounded surprised.

'It's my free Saturday and Sunday. You don't want me?''

He replied that, of course, he didn't want her. He knew that his secretary had another part-time job, that she worked in a local hospital three weekends out of four. But somehow he didn't believe that this was what she had planned for this weekend. He felt a twinge of curiosity. But she didn't usually tell him what she was doing with her spare time. Their hours together were between ten and five on all week-days except Friday when she worked late. Outside of that her life was private. He went up and put a hand on the back of a chair. She paused in her typing. 'I hope you enjoy it. You deserve a break.'

'It's not quite a holiday.' She bent over her work.

'It's hot in here.' Thomas took off his coat and hung it over the back of his chair. 'We're not the only surgery around here now, did you know that? And I don't mean doctors.' He loosened his tie. 'Anyone else out there waiting to see me?' He nodded towards the outer room.

'No, it's empty. I just looked.'

'Quiet tonight. Is that good or bad? I'll call it good.'

'It's good,' said Sheila. She laughed. 'While it lasts,' she added.

Thomas ran his fingers through his hair. He had attractive hair, sleek and thick. 'Sometimes I think we should lock this door.'

'I don't think that would look very good,' said Sheila.

Her employer laughed, but there was an edge on his laugh and Sheila averted her eyes at once.

Some time after this, after three more brief telephone calls, which did not interrupt them much, Sheila got herself a drink of water which she did not finish. 'Drink it up or pour it away,' said Thomas, 'or it'll get knocked over.'

Then the telephone rang again. This time it was a caller who did not speak.

'Just a lot of breathing,' said Thomas.

'I hate that,' said Sheila. 'I hate it when it's like that.'

'Has it happened before then?'

'Yes. Just once. When you were out. I hate it.'

'It happens,' said Thomas. 'You're meant to hate it.'

They worked for a few minutes, then Thomas said: 'I thought you said there was no one outside.'

Sheila shook her head with a smile. 'There wasn't.'

'There's someone there now. Someone's just come in.'
He straightened his tie, which had become disarranged.

'I'll go and see.' Sheila got up.

'No,' said Thomas. 'I'll go myself.' He looked serious.
'I want to see who it is.'

An insect was buzzing round the centre light. Sheila
moved toward the window to close it against the entrance
of any more. There was a line of sweat on her face.

The front door banged again and then could be heard
opening again shortly afterwards. They both heard it.
Sheila moved towards the inner door. Then she looked
back at Thomas who gave her a smile, as earlier she had
smiled at him. Between a smile and a smile sometimes a
gulf yawns.

The little clod of earth lay on a plastic saucer on a table
in the Police laboratory drying out. It had been fairly fresh
and new when placed there. It wasn't easy, the lab. said, to
be precise, but comparing the drying out rate with another
piece, they'd say that the clod of earth, when found, had
been fresh, new, young, a virgin clod, not many minutes
from the soil.

'Be strange, wouldn't it,' said Coffin, who earlier had
been reading the report, 'if that sod of earth came off the
grave of old Izzy Steinberg? Earth to earth, eh?'

'Would it?' said Dove, his imagination untitillated.

'Old Steinberg must have known something about murder. And murder in this house, too.'

'Over a hundred years ago,' said Dove sceptically. 'He
wouldn't have much to say about this one.'

'I wonder.'

'Nothing wrong with this house. Not much anyway.'

'It'll need exorcising, I should think.'

'Well, old Izzy was originally a Jew, and we don't know
about Thomas Barr. He owned the freehold, by the way.
Bought it when he moved in.'

'I thought all this land was leasehold round here,' said
Coffin, going to the window overlooking the street and
looking out. 'Belonged to the Church Estates.'

'This is a little island of freehold. Just the first half dozen houses in the street. Don't ask me why.'

The land on which the house stood and for many acres around had been associated with the Priory and Manor of St. Barnabas. Rich agricultural land and orchards had been there before houses. But like all medieval estates its land tenures were made up of complicated parcels of ownerships and right. These houses in Great Barnabas Street represented all that was left of a smallholding. The owner had held freely for himself and his heirs while himself owning some small labour services to the Priory demesne lands. He had been a villein holding free land and as the years passed his descendants counted themselves free men and forgot about the labour services and eventually made a good sale of their land when Henry VIII destroyed the monasteries.

'Some historical reason,' said Coffin, studying the scene. He was familiar with it. He could see the top of the new Police Station and the façade of the new jam factory (country-fresh jams, straight from the orchard to your table) was just beginning to appear, but otherwise the look of the streets were as he had known them over two decades. Such changes as there had been were for the better. On the whole the houses were cleaner and the paintwork brighter. Moreover, for the first time in its history, the district had an element of fashion. Several streets of the neat-fronted little early nineteenth-century houses now housed smart, expensive families. And these houses had window boxes and new iron railings and window blinds in summer. Outside stood smart cars, because although these families did not own Bentleys and Rolls they were the children of Rolls and Bentleys and frequently entertained their parents. Camilla lived in such a house. And so, for his sins, did Coffin, because his wife had bought it after making a successful film. She had then mortgaged it to make an unsuccessful one and somehow their finances had never been the same since.

As a matter of fact there was quite a theatrical element in the neighbourhood. Around the corner, and across the main road was the old Music Hall, the Regency, now a

repertory theatre, in whose founding both Thomas Barr
and John Coffin (but more reluctantly and only under
pressure from his wife) had been influential. There had
been a suggestion to re-open it as a music hall of a rather
art nouveau sort and Barr and Coffin had resisted it, Coffin
because he had enough trouble in this district without
importing any, and he could guess the sort of client such a
hall would attract.

And as well as the theatre, there was the Church Hut
where the Ballet Company rehearsed three times a week.

And then, in addition, just down the road in Great Barnabas Street, was what the neighbourhood called 'the
hostel for little boy actors'. It was, in fact, a well run house
where the juvenile students of the London Theatre School
lived in term time, travelling up to their academy every
day in a small bus. At any one time they included children
appearing in television commercials or acting in films, so
that one or two well-known if not exactly famous faces
were always among them. The hostel was run by a plump,
pretty lady who had formerly been a dancer. This little
community was both popular and unpopular according to
how well the children were conducting themselves.

'How are the kids behaving these days?' said Coffin idly.
He could see that a bright green flag had been stuck out
of one window and was fluttering in the wind.

'All docile lately. That last little batch that gave all the
trouble have gone off and this lot seem quieter. But you
can't tell. Anything could happen. This lot aren't as pretty
as the last lot, that may mean something.'

'They didn't see anything the night of the murder?'

'No. All tucked up and asleep. So they said.'

'It's remarkable how no one saw anything that night.'

'Yes, we're out of luck there. But several people have
come forward and said that over the last few weeks they
have noticed a man in the road. They're a suspicious lot
round here and they thought he was watching someone.
They thought he was a policeman, to tell you the truth.'

'Maybe nothing in it. But it could be.'

Their eyes met.

'Any guesses?' said Dove.

'A man. They thought he was a policeman,' said Coffin thoughtfully. 'How did he walk?'

'They didn't say,' said Dove. 'But I can ask.'

So, on the fourth day, Tuesday, after Thomas Barr and Sheila Daly, his secretary, were murdered, and while the newspapers were still screaming and television reporters still seeking to interview Camilla Barr, all the police knew was that:

An intruder had walked into the house in Great Barnabas Street sometime in the hours between 9 and 9:30.

He or she had shot them with a gun, so far unfound.

He, or again she, had left a piece of mud on the floor, probably from the old graveyard.

It was possible that this attacker had worn a mask.

And possibly had sat down in a chair and smoked a cigarette.

They knew this. And they also knew that they did not have Charlie Grinling.

They had to consider then three possibilities.

First, that the girl Sheila Daly was so far gone towards death that she did not know what she said.

Second, that she did know what she said and that Charlie Grinling was a real person.

Third, that she did know what she said, but that the name Charlie Grinling meant something to Sheila Daly in her private and personal work, but perhaps to no one else, and that he was going to be no help at all to a murder investigation.

This third possibility seemed the most likely of all.

'Well, now that I've captured you,' said the man to Camilla. Their interview in the sitting room of the Barr flat was proceeding.

"I wouldn't call it that.'

'It's a word that rises straight to the lips when thinking of the affairs of you and your husband. Late husband.'

'I don't know what you mean.'

'Someone was caught, weren't they?'

Camilla stood up. So did he.

'I think you'd better go now.'

'You wanted the business finished, eh? Well, I can understand that. But like I say, now I've captured you I have one or two questions to ask *you*. So far, you've done all the asking and I've done all the answering.'

'It's your job. I've paid you.'

'You're too right. You've paid once. There might be a second bill.'

'What do you mean by that?' Camilla rounded on him.

'Never mind. Leave it for the time. Get back to the questions. Start at this one: when did you get back to this country?'

'That's my business.'

'So? But as you say, you've paid me. We have a relationship. So it's my business, too.'

Camilla was silent.

'Let me tell you how you are placed,' he said. 'You are a suspect. You may have killed your husband and the girl. If you're in trouble, I'm in trouble.'

'Get out,' said Camilla.

'You thought you could do all the calling, use me as you

want, get what information you were after and then walk out. Now you see you can't do that. It looked easy for you. But I'm here to tell you that nothing is as easy as it looks.'

'I paid you.'

'For what you wanted. I'm beginning to think money wasn't enough.' He sat down. 'I'll take a drink.' Camilla hesitated. 'Whisky,' he said. 'I'll have it as part of my wages.'

'I don't know if there is any,' said Camilla, looking round. 'I've only just arrived.'

'In the cupboard on the right. Where it always was, I suppose.'

'I see you didn't waste your time.'

'Listen, I've been in and out of this place so often in the last fortnight I know it like my own.' He saw Camilla's expression. 'Oh, don't worry. It was all strictly legal, more or less.'

She poured some whisky, noting that it was a blend new to her. Silently she handed it to him.

'You'd better have some yourself.'

'I don't drink.'

'If true,' and he looked at her sceptically, "this is the time to start.'

Camilla sat down opposite him. She didn't take a drink. Defiance of some sort was necessary to her.

'Now let's start at the beginning. You got hold of me. I don't know how you found out about me, but you had my name and address ready when you needed it. Perhaps women like you always do. Martin Kelly, 23 Magellan Street. You even knew how to begin the letter. Dear Mr. Kelly, I have been recommended to you by a friend who had a little trouble with her husband.'

'I didn't say that.'

'It was what you meant. I want a politely corrupt detective to get some dirt on my husband.'

'No.'

'What you didn't tell me was that you wanted him dead.' He swallowed some of his drink. 'You've got yourself in trouble and me in there with you. I've been around this

district a lot the last weeks. I'll have been seen. Sooner or
later someone's going to mention that fact.'

This time Camilla poured herself a drink.

'Yes, you're beginning to realise what you've done now,'
he said. 'Drink a little deeper and think what you're going
to say to the police about me.'

'I didn't kill my husband,' said Camilla.

'You wrote to me from New York and asked for a day
to day report on your husband. As much detail as possible,
you said. I got this for you. I did a good job. Perhaps too
good.'

'Yes,' said Camilla. 'I admit that. You did what was
wanted.'

'I knew when you actually sent me the keys to this
apartment so I could get in and look round, that you were
in dead earnest. You wanted something, but I wasn't sure
what. I think I know now and it won't do.'

'No?'

'No. I've got a pebble in my stomach.'

Camilla stared at him.

'It means I'm scared. I've been let in for something more
than I understand.'

'You won't lose your life,' said Camilla contemptuously.

'I've got something as valuable to me as my life to lose,
lady, my livelihood. I'm going to stay around and protect
that.'

For the first time, Camilla noticed that his suit although
pressed, was old. He looked clean, muscular and very
alert, but he didn't look prosperous. His report to her in
New York had been impeccably typed, but now she saw
behind it not a large office, but his own hand. One hand
had a finger joint missing. The top of the third finger on
the left hand was gone. As he walked towards the door,
she saw he walked with a very slight roll, as if he was a
sailor, or perhaps lame in one leg.

'I'm going to stay around and find out everything. What
there was about your husband. Why you were really having him watched and what your intentions were with re-
gard to him.'

'I shan't pay you,' said Camilla coolly. 'Not for that sort of work.'

'Won't you?'

'So now I suppose you will threaten to go to the police?'

'The police!' he laughed. 'Do you think I'll have to *go* to them? Don't you think they don't know my face?'

When she was alone, Camilla went slowly round the apartment which was the top half of a small house in one of the newly smart roads of Coffin's manor. It was strange to be back in rooms she had once, but only for a little, known so well. Everything in it had been chosen by herself, and now, although it was such a little while ago, had a dated look. Perhaps it was just because she had been in New York.

Tom hadn't really done anything at all to the place, just lived here a little, kept it clean, and written to her affectionately every week, as if he expected her home soon. Had he really expected her? And had she really meant to come?

There was a photograph of them both standing on the bookcase and she picked it up and studied it. It was a good photograph of her, but it was at Thomas she looked, his face staring out at her with a smile. She remembered him smiling, she could hardly remember him without a smile. It seemed as if his lips had always that slight upward curve on them as if he was always in on a secret joke which no one else saw. She had asked him about it once, and he had said it was nothing, just the shape his lips naturally took and meant nothing, nothing else at all.

'I didn't understand you, Tom,' she said, putting the photograph down. 'And not understanding you I shouldn't have married you. But it was your fault too. You didn't understand me, didn't see how determined and ambitious I was: you thought understanding would grow with physical contact, that lips and hands and skin would help us to grasp what we couldn't get in speech. That was a stupid mistake for a clever man, Tom. Especially one whose trade was in speech and communication. Man's a talking animal when all is said and done. Maybe the words don't have to be put into speech, but they have to be there in the mind, shaping the thoughts, or there are no thoughts. It's not true people can understand each other without words, or if they do, then it's on such a level it's not worth considering.'

She had decorated the room well; design, after all, was her job, and although what she designed were tiny valuable little objects, she could do big things too. She hadn't designed the furniture, but had chosen some by a friend, a Dane called Thor. Now she thought she'd made a bad choice. It hadn't really come off.

Camilla herself designed jewelled objects, not necessarily to be worn, sometimes just to be handled. 'Like a modern Fabergé,' someone had said. 'Only in better taste,' Camilla had replied firmly. It was a sophisticated, expensive trade, and naturally New York was the home for it. Once it had been Paris, then St. Petersburg and now the place for bijoux of this elegant, slightly decadent sort was New York. London, even at its richest, had never been right for it. Too stolid, perhaps. Possibly what you needed was not a court but a fear of revolution.

Thick yellow carpets, blonde furniture, walls treated to look like gleaming wood, everything now looked second rate and not quite honest. It needed feet to scuff the walls and mark them, it wanted an air of use to the furniture and the stains of life to mark the carpet. This was still the show room in a decorated shop. Tom must have hated it.

Camilla went over to the desk, which was Swedish, and opened it. Inside she saw a bundle of her letters and almost nothing else. Like everything else in this room, Tom seemed to have avoided the desk. Except that he had marked it as Camilla's by keeping her letters there.

She held the bundle, but did not open it. Then she saw that even Tom had not opened the last three letters. He had stored them with the envelopes still sealed. Perhaps he had been saving them up for a treat. Too much love? Or too little, which did it represent? With pain, Camilla replaced them and closed the desk. There were things about people you weren't meant to know, and she had a feeling this flat was going to teach her them about Tom.

The kitchen was untidy and showed more signs of use than anything she'd seen so far. The top of the pastel

coloured stove was burnt, the edge of the matching flat sur-
faces all round were marked with burns as if Tom had lit
many cigarettes and left them smouldering. He had had a
telephone extension brought in, she saw, and around it on
the wall had scribbled telephone numbers and now mean-
ingless messages. She looked and saw embedded among
the London exchanges her own telephone number in New
York.

She stared at it. Not a smart district, but friendly as New
York went, and where she had liked to live. Not really a
home, she would never have chosen to settle there for ever,
but a stimulating and enlivening temporary settlement.
Tom had never telephoned her there; but apparently had
considered it. Perhaps he had even tried and found her
not at home.

The kitchen contained odds and ends of food, but
nothing much. Everything looked normal, but presumably
the police had been here. And she knew that Martin Kelly
had. You wouldn't have known it, though, they had left no
traces. Nor had the food, for that matter, except for the
burns on the stove. It didn't look as if Tom had done much
serious eating here. Or serious living, either. She went to
the refrigerator and looked in. A chicken pie and a packet
of chipped potatoes. Chips with everything. Frozen hard.

She went into the big bedroom. She had been careful
to decorate this in a style which would not embarrass a
man sleeping on his own, almost as if she knew she might
get up and walk out one day. Tom *had* been sleeping on
his own; she could see no sign of a woman having been
there. Perhaps there wouldn't be. Perhaps Sheila had never
been here. After all, this was careful old Tom she was
thinking about. Tom who had his career to consider.

But Tom hadn't been careful. If the signs to be read in
that room in Great Barnabas Street were true Tom hadn't
been careful at all. But this hardly seemed possible. It
wasn't in character.

Camilla sat down and stared in the mirror. 'What did
I do to you, Tom, after all, when I went away?' she said
aloud. 'And what did I do to you when I got Martin Kelly

to work on you.' Since she had no answer, her reflection naturally did not give her one, but stared back hostile and composed. But there was a stale old thought chasing itself round and round like a rat doing a laboratory trick in the back of her mind, and this thought was that somehow she had let violence in.

Behind what had happened to Tom and Sheila there had to be a moment in time when the normal crept out and violence came in. A door had opened. Either someone had opened it from the inside, or someone had given it a push from outside. It might be the hand was hers.

A hand had pushed open a door in very truth in Great Barnabas Street.

A door banged in the hall and roused Camilla. There was also a light patter of paws and she knew at once who had arrived.

'Cammy?' A light young voice called. 'Camilla?'

'In here.' She went to the door of the bedroom and looked out. 'Jen.'

'Oh, Camilla, it's lovely to see you.'

At the threshold Jen and a pale pekingese dog, both slightly breathless, were standing expectantly. Then they both rushed in. Jen was always rushing, and the dog, tethered to her, was obliged to rush too. He slowed her down slightly though, and the aggrieved looks that passed between them showed that both parties found the relationship irksome. Jen bent down and unhooked the leash. He gave himself a slight shake and walked a few yards off. Jen gave herself a slight shake too.

Jen and Camilla looked at each other. Jen had grown two inches since Camilla had seen her last and lost a lot of weight. Her hair was several shades lighter and much much longer, now it hung to her waist, straight and shining. Camilla knew how much work went into keeping hair like that.

'You've changed, Jen, grown up a lot. But oh thanks for coming.'

'Oh, it had to be me,' said Jen, putting her big handbag, which seemed to be all the luggage she had, on the floor.

She held out a bunch of house-keys. 'Want these back? No? I'll keep them. I'm so terribly sorry about this, Cammy darling. I loved Tom. He was a darling.' There were tears in her eyes.

Camilla's own eyes were dry and she drew away a little. 'I loved him too, Jen,' she said, taking a cigarette. 'But as a marriage it didn't work out. It was my fault, much more than his. I should never have gone away. I thought things would get better if we had a rest from each other, but they didn't. I suppose they got worse.'

'Suppose?' Jen's eyes were wide.

Camilla spread out her hands. 'It ended this way, didn't it? Tom dead, his secretary dead with him. I've got some blame to take for that, somehow.'

Jen looked at her steadily. 'You feel guilty, Cam, I can see that. Perhaps you are to blame for something. Personally, I do think you are to blame for leaving Tom, but he must have had something to do with it. I've known you all my life and I'd call you stable. I'm sure Tom was.'

Stories of what the room in Great Barnabas Street had looked like, and speculations about what had gone on there, were spreading in the streets. Jennifer had heard them.

'And there's someone you're forgetting who has a part in this,' said Jen shrewdly.

'Who?' Camilla stirred.

'Sheila Daly. Don't forget *she's* there. She's not *all* victim. Somewhere, somehow, she's played a positive part.'

Sheila Daly had been Thomas Barr's secretary for two years. During this time she had lived in the district and many people knew her. Bill Derby, the grocer in the store where she did her shopping, knew her as a quiet young woman whose weekly order was small. Jim Ferguson in the butcher's where she carefully chose her small joints of beef and lamb knew her as a girl who didn't use much meat, except just sometimes, when she ordered large juicy steaks, and then he astutely thought: 'boy friend'. She had no one to observe her in the ground floor flat in Hampton Road, a big main road leading into the centre of the city.

'What was she like, Jen?' asked Camilla. 'I never saw her.'

'Pretty, very pretty.'

'And as a person? Inside?'

Jen shook her head.

The two women were silent. Outside, a door banged and a car started up and moved away. The little dog barked, drawing attention to itself. It had a light baritone bark.

'The dog's new,' said Camilla.

'Oh, yes,' said Jen, her face at once going sad and frowning. 'Poor little thing. He was left in a dustbin. Just absolutely left. Dumped. I took him in at once.'

'Was it your dustbin then?'

'No, the dustmen found him. And brought him to me. He smelt terribly of dead fish.' She picked up the dog and gave it a hug. A long pink tongue shot out from the animal's expressionless face and licked her cheek: impossible to tell whether in love or hate.

'What happened to the other dog, Jen?' The last dog had been a sulky-faced spaniel with yellow teeth and bad breath.

Jen's gay young face went sad again. 'He bit my boy friend and my immigrants. I've had to put him in a home for delinquent dogs. It's terribly expensive. That's why I'm always so hard up.'

Camilla smiled. In one way or another Jen supported a large crowd of indigent and stray animals.

'And what's wrong with this one?' she asked, looking at the little creature.

'I don't know. But there'll be something. If they're mongrels usually the position's straightforward and you know where you are. But if they're pedigree and abandoned, you can bet there's something.' Jen, although an animal lover, was a realist. 'Of course, if they're female, it's that they're pregnant and once again you know where you are. But this is a dog. So I'm still in the dark. But I'll find out,' said Jen, with the confidence of long experience. 'He'll bite me or something and then I'll know.'

Camilla suddenly remembered something. 'Jen, your immigrants, what did you mean?'

'Oh, I had a family from Pakistan living with me who hadn't got permits or something important. They didn't have anywhere to live just then. But it's all right now. After the dog bit them their luck seemed to turn and now they've all got marvellous jobs and are buying a car.'

She paused. 'That reminds me—you know when the dog barked just now? It was because he heard a car. There was a man sitting in a car outside here when I came in. I think that was his car moving off. He's been here all the time. Do you think he was watching here?'

'What did he look like?'

'Of course, I couldn't see all that well. Dark hair, dark suit, sort of sombre look all round. Neat, though. The car too. Black but well polished. Do you think he was a detective?'

'Yes,' said Camilla identifying Martin Kelly. 'Yes, probably he was a detective.'

'You know him then?'

'He was here, talking to me,' said Camilla; she went to the window and looked down on the street.

'I wonder why he hung about,' said Jen, coming to join her and looking out too.

'He was suspicious. What I wonder is why he went away now?'

'Perhaps he'd seen all he wanted to see,' said Jen.

The door bell rang. Hesitantly. Then softly rang again. The hand on the bell wasn't sure of itself.

The man at the door was tall and slender and wearing dark rimmed spectacles. He had red hair and the thin skin that goes with it.

'I didn't know whether to ring the bell or not. I thought you were here. I saw you at the window.' He was always one to rush with the explanation, to tell you once, and then tell you again.

'Clem! I'm glad you did ring. Come in.' Always you had to make Clem Grove welcome, because if you didn't, nervously he might not come again. No one was ever less sure of his welcome.

'I wasn't sure if I ought to come. But I did want to see you, Camilla.'

'I'm very glad you did,' said Camilla again.

'I mean . . . in the circumstances.'

'But that's all the more reason.' A black little joke rose to her lips about how every girl ought to meet the man who had found her husband dead.

'It was awful, Camilla,' said Clement, blurting out the one thing he hadn't meant to say.

'Come in, Clem.' One of the things about Clement was that because he so often said things twice, you found yourself repeating things too. But at least his speech defect seemed to have cleared up.

Clement came in and at once fell over the dog, which barked hysterically to join in the fun.

Jen picked up the dog, and helped her cousin settle their visitor in a chair. But, although he lowered himself to the chair rather as a dog does when told to sit, he at once got up again. 'No, I can't stay. I'm really on my way to my speech training lesson.'

'You are better,' said Camilla, more to soothe him down than anything else. 'I noticed.'

'Oh yes. I'm getting on marvellously.' He sounded wretched. 'It's all in the mind, of course. Camilla, I want you to know how sorry I am about Thomas. And sorry in particular that it was me . . .' he paused.

'Someone had to find them,' said Camilla, controlling herself. 'It was hard on you too.'

'You are marvellous.'

'Some time I'd like to talk to you about it. I'd *like* to talk to you about it. I'd like you to tell me.'

'If that's what you really want.' He sounded unhappy at the thought.

'I've been to the house. Now I'd like to know how it was when you got there,' said Camilla.

'Goodbye for now then, Camilla.' He held her hand for a moment. 'I have to go now. I mustn't be late.' He went away, first falling over the dog again.

'I wonder where he goes for his speech training,' observed Camilla.

'Oh he goes to old Mark Berkeley, you know, he lives at the hostel for the little boy actors.'

'He used to be an actor too?'

'Well, in the old Music Halls, when they existed. I believe he had been on the straight stage once. He had a ventriloquist act with a dummy. I suppose that does help you to teach speech training.' She moved into the kitchen. 'I'll get some food. You put your feet up and rest. I brought some food round from Fortnum and Mason's.' Jen never had any money, but she believed in shopping for the best.

'Poor old Clem,' said Camilla, 'he couldn't say boo to a goose, and it had to be him that found them.'

'Did you really want him to tell you all about it,' said Jen. She was deftly preparing a meal, whipping up an omelette, arranging a salad. Camilla was watching her with her taste-buds unstimulated. In the world where she was living, food and drink were not what nourished you.

'Oh yes,' said Camilla, thinking about Martin Kelly. Facts, hard facts, facts about Tom and Sheila, *those* were what fed you.

As soon as they were at the table the telephone rang. Camilla sat without moving.

'You should answer that,' said Jen.

'I don't want to answer it.'

'Shall I take it?'

'No.' Camilla got up. 'I will.'

She picked up the telephone and stood there holding it in front of the wall with all the numbers scrawled on it. MO 2-1670, that was a New York number, her own and the others, like 01.8967. Maybe that was Sheila's.

'Hello,' she said. 'Camilla Barr speaking.'

'Yes, I can hear you,' said Martin Kelly in an angry voice. 'And what I want to say is: don't think you can get away with it. I saw, I tell you, I saw.'

'Get away with it? What is this?' Camilla sensed a feeling in him, as if he had at last discovered something about her. She was puzzled and afraid. 'What do you see?'

'You don't mind who you are, do you? Or who you take down with you. Well, I'll have something to say about that. And it'll take some talking. Don't try to wriggle out. I'll fix it when we have to meet. And there will be meetings. At a time and for a purpose arranged by me.'

'Are you trying to blackmail me?' said Camilla.

'Blackmail, yes, that's the word. Blackmail,' said Martin Kelly. 'Think about *that* when you go to bed tonight.'

INTERLUDE

But Camilla was right about the mealy-mouthedness. What was breaking all round them could be a great scandal. Already people were saying it could break up the pattern of politics. And it was true. Or there was a chance it could be true. Although no one yet knew it, an American politician was going to be involved.

Some thousands of miles away in Washington, D.C., William Walpole, U.S. Senator, banged down his bags in his apartment. He was home.

'Hi,' he called.

His very young wife came running out to greet him, bathrobe flying. She left it open on purpose; she was anxious to do her duty as a wife.

'You're back,' she said.

'As soon as I could,' he said enthusiastically.

'And you saw your mother? And got what you wanted?'

'Yes.'

His purpose in visiting his mother had been to interview a young cousin as his secretary. Since his last secretary had left he had been managing with temporaries. Not a satisfactory expedient, for a man of his standing. It was his mother who suggested that he 'keep it in the family'. It was her family.

'I expect you'll be glad to get back to Barbara,' his mother had said, watching his preparations to depart.

'Yes.'

'Dear Barbie,' said his mother, somewhat less than warmly.

Barbie was now watching him expectantly.

'Yes,' he repeated. 'Cousin Beattie's coming.'

'What's her other name? You won't call her Cousin Beattie?'

'Not while she's working, no,' said the Senator reassuringly; he knew his Barbara had a jealous edge on her. He liked it. And she liked that he liked it, so they were all happy. 'She's Mrs. Bibby. Been widowed for about two years.'

'Oh,' Barbie nodded. 'Oh well, I'm glad for you. I know it's been difficult since Joe Wolf went.'

Joe Wolf had been the last permanent secretary. 'You were fond of him weren't you?'

'He was a good boy. I won't get a better worker. But to tell the truth, I never thought I saw clean through him to the bottom.'

'And now he's in Europe?'

'Yes. Studying politics there. I helped him get a research grant. He had the qualifications, as you know.'

'We never met, remember,' said Barbara. She smoothed her dressing gown. 'Your breakfast's ready, why don't you come and have it and settle in.'

'Coming,' said her husband. He pushed up his newspaper and read the big news first. He knew it anyway. He was a well informed man. Then his eye fell on a short paragraph about Thomas Barr's death. He'd never met Barr. He closed the paper, and turned his attention to the day and the week ahead of him. Various little chores like replacing his personal assistant lay ahead of him, but from here the picture looked good.

On Wednesday the police suspected that Camilla Barr had had a man in her flat. On Friday morning they had a strong fix on his name and identity.

They had started from the moment of the telephone call made by Coffin to Camilla. A watch was kept on Camilla. The watchers reported that she was staying home and getting no visitors. They were not able to tap her phone. It looked like no progress, but Coffin suggested a way forward.

'We do have something to go upon: a man was seen several times in Great Barnabas Street in the week before the killing. He was a stranger and he was trying not to be noticed. And we do have something to go on: he walked badly, perhaps he was limping.'

'I see who you're getting at,' said Dove. 'I thought of him too.'

'Photograph?'

'I expect I can lay my hands on one. Previous the limp, though.'

'Of course.'

Method combined with good guessing brings results. On Thursday detectives had visited houses in Great Barnabas Street with a photograph of the man Coffin believed to be the one seen hanging about in the days before the killing.

This had a result which Dove himself had gone to confirm, not without a secret satisfaction of his own; he had an old score to settle.

Dove called at a house in Great Barnabas Street. He put a few pointed questions and showed the photograph again.

'Yes, that was him. Interesting face, isn't it?' This was

his best witness, a plump elderly householder with long-range eyes.

'Very interesting,' said Dove, pocketing the photograph.

'I thought to myself: interesting face to make up for the stage. It would photograph well too. And now you say he's a criminal.' She sounded disappointed.

'I didn't say so.'

'Oh.' She looked from the photograph to Dove's face. 'Oh, well, I'd have given him more than a walking-on part myself. Anyway, he's the one I saw. He hung around for some days on and off. Thought no one saw him.' She smiled. 'Is he your boy friend then?'

'No,' said an outraged Dove.

'You've got his photograph. No need to be upset. You look old enough to be a consenting adult to me.' She giggled, baiting him deliberately. She even waited hopefully for him to join in the giggle, but he didn't. '*Now*, Mrs. Tritton,' he said.

'Well, it's him. I saw him,' she said. 'That's what you wanted, isn't it?'

'That's what I wanted.'

This was the result of guessing. Method checked in the street where Thomas Barr lived and Camilla now stayed and produced another witness who had seen this man there too.

'Came out about twenty minutes after Mrs. Barr went in the day she arrived. I was on the watch. Interested, you see. Then he got in a car and sat for a bit. Then he drove away. No, he hasn't been back. Not while I've been watching.' The speaker was an invalid man of about thirty, crippled by a progressive paralysis. He spend most of his day in the sunlit bay window of the house opposite the Barrs' apartment. 'I was interested in him. I thought he might be a detective to tell you the truth. I read a lot of them. And I thought: he looks like something out of Raymond Chandler. He came here once, you know, Chandler, I mean. And he looked at No. 23 and went and studied the Steinberg grave in the old cemetery. He said it was one of the mysteries of the nineteenth century and that South London was the best place for real mysterious death. That was what Raymond Chandler said. At least, I think it was him. It looked like him.'

He looked wistful as Dove departed. Nature may emulate art but is never so satisfying.

From the old graveyard, where perhaps the murderer had walked before his deed, you could just see the house in Great Barnabas Street. One hundred and fifty years ago it hadn't been a long journey for the Steinberg family to go to their burial. In fact their coffins had been carried across the road on the shoulders of neighbours. Thomas Barr and Sheila Daly would have to go further to their burying. Thomas was being quietly buried on Friday and Sheila, who seemed to have no family, few friends, soon after. Camilla Barr would attend both funerals. So would about twenty thousand other people and several television cameras.

From the old graveyard from which you could see Great Barnabas Street you could also see the new Police Station, if you turned your head right and faced the other way. It was a tall, thin building faced with cream stone. All the glass in the front of it glittered in the sun. From his window John Coffin could see the trees in the old burying place and beyond the Museum and then the red brick of Great Barnabas Street.

But this Friday morning a week after Thomas Barr and his secretary Sheila Daly had been found dead, he wasn't looking out of his window. Friday was always a busy day for administrative reasons, with forms and lists to fill in. Not all his Friday troubles were strictly professional, his family seemed to produce crises on Friday for some reason or another. Today for instance he was supposed to come back home having decided between four nursery schools for his young son, and having viewed at least two of them. *That* was out for a start.

On the table in front of him he had a selection of photographs. There was Camilla Barr in a formal posed picture, a copy of which her husband had kept on his desk. There was a picture of Sheila Daly on her wedding day, smiling and plump. A picture of Sheila Daly leaving the inquest on her husband. A big blown-up picture of Thomas Barr shaking hands with his agent on the night he had been returned to Parliament. Then there was a picture of Thomas and Sheila stretched across the floor of the room in which they had been found dead. This must be the picture burnt on the retina of Clement Grove.

He moved these pictures round on his desk as if to make something coherent out of them. Nothing so far.

Dove gave his quick knock on the door which meant: I'm coming in whatever you say, and was in the room. The effect on Dove of the new building seemed to have been to hurry him up. Coffin could remember when he had been a relatively slow-moving man, now he was getting brisker every day. He had a new image of himself and was trying to live up to it.

Dove started talking before he had the door closed.

'I'm telling you the truth. So we know who she's been seeing.'

'Describe him to me.'

'He's six feet one inch tall. He has dark hair and blue eyes. Fair skin. Walks with a limp. He was born 18 July, 1933. Unmarried.'

Coffin looked up and their eyes met. 'Martin Kelly. Camilla Barr and Martin Kelly. I thought it was him somehow. Now why was she using him?'

'He's been an angry man ever since he got that leg wound,' said Dove.

'For which I don't blame him,' said Coffin.

'He's a good detective, though.'

'Was.'

Once again their eyes met. 'I was never quite sure about him, even when he was with us,' said Coffin. 'Since you mention it. I always thought he might be just the nicest bit bent. I think there's not much he wouldn't risk doing now. I'm not dead sure, though. That's the trouble. I never *was* sure of him, one way or another.' He went back to fidgeting with his photographs. Camilla, Thomas, Sheila Daly. There had to be an arrangement that satisfied him.

'He wasn't easy to read,' agreed Dove. 'Isn't, I mean. He's not dead. Out there, hobnobbing with Camilla Barr. He returned to his office last night. Could be he'd been with her. Was with her when you rang. Since then, he's been back watching the flat where she is. He's been backward and forward.' He paused.

'What else have you got, then?' asked Coffin, who knew him.

'I had his photograph shown round door to door in Great Barnabas Street and Museum Street and Exhibition Road. He'd been seen there. He'd been seen a lot lately in Great Barnabas Street. That's how I got on to him. He's been noticed.'

'Watching Thomas Barr for his wife?' speculated Coffin aloud. 'Could be. Wonder how she got on to him?'

'He advertises.'

'So he does. And now he's watching her. Doesn't suggest mutual trust, does it?'

'Think they've had some sort of quarrel? I wouldn't want to go across him, the way he is now,' said Dove slowly.

'I wonder why she wanted him to watch her husband? And for what?'

'The usual,' said Dove. 'I mean, what else is there?'

'She seems so cold, as if she didn't care a damn.'

'It's beginning to look as if she was burning up inside, though,' said Dove. He said it as if it tasted wry in his mouth. No woman had ever burned up inside on account of him. 'I still don't see how she's got across Martin Kelly.'

'Unless he thinks she killed her husband. He wouldn't thank her for getting him into that kind of mess. But even so . . .'

'Unless he *knows* she did,' said Dove.

They looked at each other.

'Knows? Yes,' said Coffin thoughtfully. 'If he'd been watching the house in Great Barnabas Street perhaps he saw more than he was meant to.' He reached out for the telephone. 'We must talk to Mr. Kelly.'

Mr. Kelly was out of the way though; he often was. His office, small and bleak, was there, but empty; he had no secretary. But this absence confirmed Coffin in his belief that with Martin Kelly things were, somehow, wrong, all wrong. No one seemed to know where he was living. Out in the wilderness of one of the south-east suburbs, it was thought. He was unmarried.

But even if Martin Kelly had been located on that Friday morning, Coffin would not have been free to see him. He had got to attend first the inquest and then the funeral of Thomas Barr. Subsequently he would quietly attend Sheila Daly's. He didn't believe the old legend that the murderer couldn't keep away from the obsequies of his victims, but it was worth a look.

The inquest was a polite formality and the Police had already agreed to the burial of both victims taking place afterwards.

'Suppose Kelly comes to Barr's funeral,' said Dove.

'I'll talk to him then. But I doubt if he'll be there.'

Camilla smiled at him without speaking as they met leaving the church. She smiled again as she got into a car to drive away. 'There'll be a Memorial Service for my husband later,' she said to Coffin. 'If you'd like to come. There'll be an announcement.' Then her cousin started the car and they drove away. She was going to the second funeral of the day.

'What about Sheila Daly?' said Coffin to Dove. 'Will there be a Memorial Service for her?' as they too drove off.

'You don't like Mrs. Barr?' said Dove, as if it came as a surprise to him.

'I think she's a very attractive and beautiful woman. And she frightens me a bit. She's one of those people who let violence in.'

Dove looked sceptical. There weren't people like that in the world for him. Only the innocent and the proved guilty, the dividing line between the two was a legal fiction, no one was wholly innocent in his world although a good many were wholly guilty.

'You means she's selfish?' he said.

'No. Something bigger and much more neutral than that. It may even be a virtue.'

'I wonder if she did kill her husband?'

'I don't know. She's beginning to look as if she thinks she did.' And it was true Camilla had looked tired and haunted. 'Of course if she's got Kelly on her tail, she's right to look worried.'

'Any more 'phone calls?' Jen asked Camilla later that day.

'Yes, a good many,' said Camilla. 'People are trying to be kind. It's tiring though.'

'I mean those you don't like getting,' said Jen dryly. 'I've noticed. I noticed the first evening.'

'Yes, there are one or two like that.'

'I mean the *man*,' said Jen.

'No, he's been quite quiet,' said Camilla faintly.

'Did you notice all the flowers for Sheila Daly? There were hardly any people but all those flowers.'

'I sent the flowers,' said Camilla. 'They were from me. I wanted her to have something.'

'And the violets?'

'No, I didn't send violets.'

'Did you notice all the flowers?' said Dove to his chief. 'Lovely, weren't they? Sickly smell, though.'

'I liked the violets,' said Coffin. He was quiet.

'I didn't see them."

'Clumps of blue.'

Although a certain number of people from the neighbourhood attended both funerals, Clement Grove didn't. He would have liked to go. It would have seemed decent to pay his respects, but he was shy. Publicity was never his thing. He sent flowers, though. Blue ones. Violets.

During the morning he worked in the Museum, where he was alone. A new assistant had been appointed but had not yet arrived. Meanwhile Clem was assessing his stock and planning a new display. From being the dustiest museum in London, it was going to be the brightest. Ideas of how you should set out a museum had changed in the last ten years, and Clem, who had visited the Rijks Museum in Amsterdam, knew what he had to do.

He looked at his watch. Time for his speech training lesson. Morning ones were unusual, but Mark Berkeley had asked for this one. He wanted to work on Clem's power of throwing his voice. Sometimes Clem thought that Mark wanted to turn him into a ventriloquist. He began to hurry: he dare not be late.

'I'm not late, am I?'

'No. No, today you're punctual.' The assent was grudging. It was very difficult to please Mark. Not in all moods nor all days, but sometimes, sometimes Mark was hell.

'I couldn't help being late the other day.'

'Punctuality is the royal virtue, my boy. Never forget that. Any public performer has to be punctual. It's part of his duty to his public. You are now a public performer.'

Clem blinked. He had graduated. Yesterday his teacher had been grumbling about projecting his voice properly; today he was a public performer. Sometimes he thought Mark forgot what he was actually training him to do. 'I may not go into actual political life. I'm in the process of changing my mind on that. I shall always do backroom work, of course. It was only while Thomas was alive, he inspired me.' Inspiration wasn't really the word. Thomas set a standard. But Thomas was dead. And the desire to equal, even surpass, had died away.

'I hope you are serious about the work we do together,' said Mark Berkeley, beginning to get huffy. He took himself seriously.

'Of course, of course.' It would never do to get Mark cross. Clem feared his teacher somewhat. 'And you've done me so much good.' This was true. Mark, although no theoretician, did know a great deal about using the voice and more by force of character than anything else he had knocked some of the hesitancy out of Clem's speech.

'Now get up, go to the window, face the wall and throw your voice so it hits the wall high up. Say "EH, EH, EH".'

Clem got up at once and started to throw his voice towards the wall as he was asked.

'Imagine it bouncing off that round spot on the wall-paper.'

'Yes,' panted Clem, at once seeing his voice meeting that round spot (it was a stain) and floating away again like a great bubble.

'Now bring it back close to you. Your voice is just above your head.'

'Yes,' said Clem. Now his voice was floating up above his head like a halo. There was no doubt Mark had an ascendency over him.

'Have you learnt your piece?'

There was a certain Victorian element to these lessons. Clem had a piece to learn which he must then recite. There was even a hint of punishment, if the piece wasn't learnt correctly.

'Yes,' said Clem. He does do me good, he reminded himself. I've really benefitted. I don't stumble at all when I speak now. Or hardly ever. I could probably go into public life now, in spite of what Tom used to say. Used to say and would never say again. 'That is, I haven't quite learnt it *all*. I thought I'd read it. I can still do my voice exercises, you know.'

He began.

Mark watched him, taking a grim pleasure in hearing him do it badly.

'You'll have to strengthen those diaphragm muscles,' he said at the end of it. 'You've got a weak thorax, lad. Never do well in character parts with a weak thorax. In fact, I doubt if you'll ever have much range.'

'I'm not trying to be a character actor. You were never on the legitimate stage yourself, were you?' said Clem. Anger had to break through their relationship sometimes.

Mark fixed him with a steady eye. 'Grave digger, followed by Horatio, followed by Hamlet at the Liverpool Queen's (the *old* Queen's). Later Macbeth and Sir Percy Blakeney in Denby. Trigorin and Teddy Luton, Leeds, followed by Maurice Tabret in *The Sacred Flame*—a lot of Maugham about then in the provinces, London was rather off him.' He smiled blandly. 'Just some of my best performances, my dear, show you the cuttings. I started off with Trelawny of the Wells, like we all did at dear old Miss Tree's Academy.'

'That would make you about ninety-six,' said Clem nastily. Perhaps Mark *was* ninety-six.

'Ninety-nine,' said Mark calmly. 'My rheumatism's bad

too, today. I shall have to pop over and see John Plowman. He's been having some good results. I find him very helpful.'

'Well, is there anything more?' said Clem; he dared to get up to go.

'No, not now, not today.' Mark sat back and watched Clem, his pupil, depart. Mark was wearing a neat brown suit and a flowered cravat. He had a slight but definite sun-tan which came, in winter from a lamp, and in summer from the sun itself. He had plenty of time to devote to his appearance. Then, 'Come back,' he called. Obediently, Clem came. 'Tomorrow we will have an extended lesson.'

'I don't need an extended lesson,' said Clem; he knew those extended lessons. They went on for far too long and left him exhausted.

'This one's for my benefit,' said his teacher. 'I've had a few good ideas and want to try them out on you. You're my guinea pig.'

'I might not be able to come tomorrow. I think I may be going down with something. I don't feel quite well.'

'Of course, I won't make a charge.'

'As a matter of fact, I haven't paid for a long while,' said Clem.

'No hurry. I'll send in the bill.' He smiled.

Now what part's he acting, thought Clem, worry scuttling round in his mind like a mouse. Svengali? Maybe Dr. Caligari?

'I'll see if I can make tomorrow,' said Clem, departing.

'You do,' smiled Mark.

'Old ventriloquist,' said Clem, quite loudly. Anger, again.

'I'm more than that. I'm a conjurer.'

'What's *that* mean?' Clem turned round at the door.

'I'm a conjurer in the old-fashioned sense. I make the dead speak.'

Clem looked back at him from the door.

'Wait.' Mark went to a cupboard in one corner of the room and from a deep long shelf took out the figure of a dummy. 'I keep it lying flat,' he said, his voice muffled by bending down. 'I might try hanging him up, but some-how I'd rather think of him resting than hanging.' What he had extracted was a masculine figure, limp of limb and lolling of neck. Mark sat down on an upright chair and propped the figure against him. It had a round vacant face with shiny eyes and a bright red mouth.

The two faces looked at Clem. 'Hello, Clem,' said the bright red mouth. 'Long time no see.'

'Oh God,' said Clem.

'Let's have a conversation,' said red mouth. 'You and me.'

'No. Please.'

'Say how do you do, like a good boy,' urged Mark Berkeley.

'How do you do, like a good boy,' said red mouth. Rather terribly, Clem thought.

'Shall we tell him a story?'

'Yes, let's tell him a story.'

'Don't bother,' said Clem.

'Let's tell him the story of Goldilocks and the Three Bears,' said Mark. 'Let's tell him about Goldilocks whose hair wasn't so very golden but who certainly deserved to be locked up, and the three bears, Big, Small and Smaller, who wanted to eat her up.'

'That's not a fairy story, that's a true story,' shrilled red mouth.

'Stop him talking like that,' said Clem. 'He gives me the creeps.'

'Yes, he is a creepy little fellow, aren't you, Charlie?' said Mark, patting the dummy's curly head.

Red mouth laughed.

'You frightened him, boy,' said Mark, as the door banged behind Clem and his feet ran down the stairs.

'*We* frightened him.'

'I'll have to put you back in the cupboard if you're not a good boy.'

'It's up to you,' said the figure jauntily. 'But why don't you and me have a talk?'

'We might.' Mark scratched his head. 'Only I don't

know what you could say that I haven't heard already.' He paused. 'Cue for laugh,' he said.

There was no audience to laugh so they did it themselves. The red mouth moved, and the noise came from Mark.

'A rehearsal?'

'A rehearsal.'

'Right.' Mark settled back in his chair. 'Let's make it our Grade A beginning. I hear you've been a bad boy lately.'

'Me a bad boy?'

'Yes, a very bad boy.'

'What did I do?'

'You were very rude to Mr. Mummery, the Mayor.'

'How was I rude?'

Mark broke off the dialogue. 'That was the point where we either had 'em rolling with laughter already, or they were getting ready to throw tomatoes.' He sat thinking. Then he raised his head.

'Goldilocks,' said red mouth.

'No, boy, no. Goldilocks, no. Keep Goldilocks out.'

'Izzy?'

'All right. Izzy?'

He paused, then said: 'Is he who?'

'Izzy, Izzy,' said the dummy in a triumphant giggle.

Mark's landlady came fussing in to the room with his clean linen. She pursed her lips at the sight of the large doll on the bed. 'Why don't you give that up?' she said. 'No future there, Mark, honestly.'

'I enjoy it.'

'I know you do.' She patted his shoulder with sympathy. 'But we've got to face it, as performers you and I are old hat.'

Sheila Daly's skin had been very white and covered with the fine golden hair, down almost, of the real blonde. She was so fair the hairs were unnoticeable to all except the pathologists who examined her in death. But in fact she had more than most people. The hairs upon her skin were dense but fine.

For a time the scientist who had prepared the report for Coffin on Sheila's dead body pondered whether he should add certain observations to his report. He did not add them, but as the piece of earth found in the room where she had died crumbled in its white sterile saucer on his bench, he continued to think about it.

Finally he visited Coffin, who was a friend. It was an unofficial private call, which took place in John Coffin's house. It was also a late night call.

'I didn't know whether to bother you with it or not. In the end I decided I would. Just something that puzzled me.'

'Come on in, Eric.' Eric Weller was a well-known fusser, heading any day now for his first ulcer. However, he was a meticulous, trained observer and had already helped Coffin once before. 'Last time you crawled out from your benches and did that for me, two years ago, it was, we got a killer who hated the human race and was levelling up with it by hitting old ladies on the head and then raping them.'

'He didn't hate the human race,' said Eric, who was also an amateur psychologist. 'It was himself he hated.'

'You said that at the time. I didn't believe it then, I don't now.'

They sat down on the pale leather Bauhaus chairs which were Mrs. Coffin's current line in furnishing. As the chairs were built for people with short legs their knees came forward rather prominently.

'Did you know that the skin supports a large population of micro-organisms? No, I don't suppose you've ever thought about it. The skin has a world of its own, in fact, with its own soil and flora and fauna.'

Coffin scratched his arm vigorously.

'Scientists call it an ectosystem; that is a world with its own balanced population living in equilibrium together.'

Coffin shifted in his chair, uneasy at the thought of the world he was carrying around on his back.

'Everyone has much the same sort of population of organisms, we're all human beings after all, and we all have the same temperature and the same degree of acidity in the skin. The population density varies, of course, between what someone has called the heavily populated forest of the axila and the sparsely inhabited desert of the forearm.'

'Not to mention the rapidly thinning and cooling forest on my scalp,' said Coffin, running his hand through it. 'I'm getting a lot more sunlight through there these days. What's that doing to the indigenous population?'

'You haven't got much to worry about. You've still got plenty of vegetation there,' said Eric. 'Plenty of bacteria, I'd say.'

'Thanks.'

'And then the bacteria are hosts in themselves to viruses. Bacteriophages, we call them. Worlds within worlds. Beautiful, isn't it? Perhaps the whole of our universe is nothing more than the itch on the skin of a giant.'

'It often feels like it,' said Coffin.

'I'm dead keen on bacteria myself. It's not strictly speaking my job, but I can extend my job. I play little games testing for bacterial traces, growing them, matching them up. Some eat one sort of thing, some another. They have tastes like anything else.'

'You make them sound real friendly.'

Suddenly Eric Weller came running right out with what he had to say. 'I wanted to tell you that I found a streak of bacteria on the girl's skin. Not such bacteria as would normally live there. But I matched it with bacteria from the specimen of soil also found in the room. She must have been in contact with that soil. Or the soil with her.'

'How do you suggest?'

'It could have been on someone's hands. Or on her hands,' said Eric.

'And where was the bacteria?' asked Coffin.

'On her thighs and belly.'

'In God's name what did happen in that room that night?' said Coffin. The picture had never been nice and with every piece of fresh information it seemed to get nastier.

Camilla Barr had received a telephone call from Martin Kelly. On this point she had lied to Jenny. The call had come late at night when her cousin was asleep and she had not wakened, although the peke had.

'Meet me Saturday, at nine in the evening at the Silver Lily—that's the Chinese restaurant in the New Cut behind the Blue Anchor.'

'I know it.' The Silver Lily was an *old* Chinese restaurant, not one of the new wave. Camilla and Thomas had gone there to eat fried rice and sweet and sour prawns in the first months of their marriage. In fact certain tones of unhappiness and desolation were now associated in Camilla's mind with fried rice. 'Yes, I know where. Don't count on me being there, though. Why should I come?'

'Because we have to talk about the night your husband died. You have to tell me what *you* know, and then I can tell you what I know. We can put our cards on the table.'

Camilla put the receiver down on his voice. She did go. She went into the Silver Lily at fifteen minutes past nine on the Saturday evening, a wet night. He wasn't there. Perhaps he had already come and gone. But she waited. And waited.

Martin Kelly did not come. She had plenty of time to think about what had happened that night her husband died.

8

On that evening, now a week ago, Thomas Barr and Sheila his secretary had worked side by side on work which interested them both. Thomas trusted Sheila without examining very much the motives for his trust. He just knew that he did so. It was perhaps a physical thing that she had big blue eyes with a direct gaze, that she moved quietly and gently, that she had a good sense of timing and never let him down.

After they had worked and discussed Sheila's holiday (which she said was not quite a holiday) and congratulated each other on the surgery waiting room being quiet (which it was, yet not so quiet as they supposed), Tom said,

'Sometimes I think we ought to lock the door,'

'I don't think that would look very good,' said Sheila.

Thomas laughed, and since it wasn't the sort of laugh he usually gave, nor one she cared to hear, the girl looked up at once.

She saw her employer leaning close to her desk. A tiny bead of sweat had formed on his brow. He put out a hand and started to rummage on her desk.

'Where is it? You always keep some aspirin there, don't you?'

'Yes.' Sheila found the bottle and he swallowed two tablets without waiting for water.

'I expect you're wondering why I laughed like that?'

'No!' Sheila shook her head. It was a warning but he chose not to hear it.

'I think my wife's having me watched.'

'You *think*?'

'I know she is.'

They stared at each other.

'What is it she wants to know?' asked Sheila.

'What is it that wives usually want to know?' He had moved a little way away again. 'But why she *should,* that's the question, isn't it?'

Sheila eyed him.

'I mean who's been telling her things? Someone has been giving her ideas. She thinks I'm up to something.'

'I can't bear to hear you talk like that. Not with that note in your voice. It's beneath you.'

'Yes, you set a high store on my dignity, don't you, Sheila?' And when she still didn't answer: 'And so do I *not.*'

Sometime after this, after three telephone calls which did not disturb them, Sheila got herself a drink of water.

There was another telephone call which Sheila answered. The caller did not speak, only breathed heavily. This she disliked and said so.

They had some time of peace then, until Thomas said, 'I thought you said there was no one outside?'

Sheila shook her head with a slight smile. 'There wasn't.'

He went to see who it was.

An insect was buzzing round the centre light. Sheila moved towards the window as if to close it against the entrance of any more. There was a line of sweat on her face.

She sat down and put a hand to her head.

'My dear,' said Thomas, turning back to her.

'I'm sorry.' She put her head right down. 'I feel sick.'

'I'm sorry, terribly sorry to have involved you in all this.'

'No. Not you, it's me,' she mumbled. 'Don't you see that. Me.' She sat up.

'Are you feeling faint?' He moved to her side.

'No, it's my hands. They've got dirt on them.'

The front door banged again. They both heard it.

'Don't say anything,' said Thomas. 'Don't, don't say anything.'

9

So on the eighth day what the police knew was very little more than they had known on the fourth day. But they had a new relationship to study: the relationship between Camilla Barr and Martin Kelly.

One of the other lines of inquiry was to interview the firm which had painted the window frames in the house in Great Barnabas Street. Poulton's of Lazarus Street.

The two men who had painted the room were called John Annett and Charles Colver. It was the boy Charles Colver who had actually painted the window. Coffin interviewed him. His mate John Annett had gone into hospital three days before the murder and was still there.

'You'd better see him yourself,' Dove had said.

'Oh. Got a record on him, have we?'

'No.' Dove shook his head. 'But as soon as I saw him I remembered I'd questioned him about the girl who was abducted six months ago in Dover Road. Carried off, clothes stripped off and left in the country.'

'We never got the man who did it,' said Coffin thoughtfully.

'It probably wasn't him. He seemed clear at the time. Could prove he was with friends, that sort of thing. But it's worth bearing in mind. You might read something on his face.'

Coffin smiled.

'As a matter of fact, I've always thought the girl in Dover Road knew who did it to her. Knew him real well. Drove him to it and knew it.'

'She probably did,' said Coffin.

'So you see him yourself. And after all he *is* called

Charles. And the girl before she died was talking about a Charlie.'

'Exactly.'

Charles was young, smiling and friendly. 'Yes, I did a bad job painting the window first time round,' he said. 'Not my fault. I'd had a rotten time with the girl friend and I couldn't keep my mind on my job.' He smiled broadly: all things must be forgiven to him, he implied. 'And then you see John was ill and couldn't keep an eye on me. He's supposed to keep an eye on me.' Charles was about eighteen, and young with it.

'And then you went back and did it again?'

'The customer complained. And when the boss told me about the complaint I admitted I'd done it bad. It's always best to tell the truth, I reckon.'

'It depends who has to pay in the end.'

'Well, it wasn't going to be me; I'm only an apprentice.'

'Were you alone the second time round?'

'What d'you mean?'

'With John Annett being ill and you knowing the place, I thought perhaps they didn't send anyone with you that time,' said Coffin, smiling in his turn. Two could play at the game of innocence.

'Well, no, they didn't.'

'So you were alone.'

'Yes.'

'You don't sound convinced.'

'I was alone.'

'I suppose Sheila Daly was working there.'

'Who's Sheila Daly?'

'She was Mr. Barr's secretary.'

'Oh, yes, that bird. Yeah, she was there, I suppose, flipping in and out. I didn't really notice.'

'Nice looking girl, wasn't she?'

'I didn't really notice.'

'Did you speak to her at all?'

'She was inside and I was out.'

'Did you go inside?'

Colver hesitated. 'She made a cup of tea and offered me one.'

'So you did speak to her?'

'That was all.'

'But you noticed her?'

'She was a little old for me,' said Colver. 'I know exactly what you're getting at and no, I didn't come back one little odd evening and beat her up.'

'Are you ever called Charlie?' asked Coffin.

For the first time, Colver looked surprised and the smile wore off. 'No,' he said. 'They always call me Check.'

The background of Check Colver was gone over. His mates at work and his family were talked to, but nothing stood out. Check was not good, but he wasn't strikingly bad, either. And if suspicion had hovered over his head once or twice nothing had ever been proved.

A policewoman called on Check's mother with a pretext about the electoral roll which deceived Check's mother, who was a simple, if sinful, woman.

Even to the girl, Joan Eames, a stranger to her, she seemed anxious for her sins to find her out.

'There's three men in this house all of an age to vote, dear,' she said to Joan.

'And their names?' said Joan briskly.

'Colver. I'm Mrs. Colver. And there's not one of 'em knows their own father. I don't, I'm telling you that, so how should they? Perhaps they're really called Murphy or Parker or Smith. I think there's one of them could be called Polowski if every one had their due, but who's to tell? Some things you can't really tell, dear, and that's one of them.'

'I'll just put down Colver,' said Joan stolidly. 'Christian names?'

'William, John and Charles.'

'Charlie?' said Joan, her pencil poised.

'Char*les*. We always call him Check.'

Charles never called Charlie, wrote Joan. This was one of the things she'd been sent to find out. See if they ever call him Charlie, they'd told her. She'd found out.

'I was a wicked woman to my husband while he was alive,' said Mrs. Colver. 'And now he's dead, he's come back to haunt me.'

'Really?' She's a nut, Dove had said. Mrs. Colver's a nut, we all know that. But he hadn't told her why.

'I pay for my misdeeds. Oh yes. All those favours I refused my husband when he was alive he comes back now and takes. Every night, yes.' She smacked her lips.

Lonely, widowed women get these fantasies, said Joan to herself. But Mrs. Colver didn't look frustrated. She looked thoroughly happy, as though Mr. Colver was at last being a success.

'I don't know why you're telling me this,' said Joan Eames.

'I'm telling you because you appear to be a girl that wants to know things,' said Mrs. Colver, with what appeared to be a touch of clairvoyance. 'And don't tell me that's not the case.'

On the way out, Joan Eames was stopped by a neighbour of the Colvers who had been working in her front garden.

'Forgive me stopping you, but I couldn't help seeing you talking to her at the front door and I know the things she says. Don't believe a word of it. Maybe she was a bit of a bad girl in the war, but that's a long time ago, isn't it? And she looked after the old man like he was a baby before he died. And he was helpless for a long time. Just like a log he was, poor fellow. I think she went a bit funny then. She was ever such a nice looking woman then, you wouldn't think so now to look at her, would you?'

'No,' said Joan Eames. 'No, you wouldn't.'

The strange sad life of Check Colver was unveiled a little, as so often happens in murder investigations, where the lives of the most ordinary citizens seem beyond belief.

He had a brother who had married five years ago and moved two streets away; he was called Ted and was not in the roll call of names Mrs. Colver had assembled. Ted said he didn't want to have anything to do with what went on in that household. He'd married and moved away and was a free man now and he advised all his brothers to do the same. They were all crackers round there and always would be while their mother held sway. *She* was the one that did it. But he had to admit that of them all Check was as sane as any. Considering everything round there.

'What goes on that's so strange then?' asked Joan Eames. She was curious on her own account now, as well as professionally.

The brother scratched his head. 'Hard to know where to begin. It's all little things. I mean when you're there, inside, it doesn't seem so bad, it's only when you're outside looking back, like I am, you say, surely it wasn't really like that. Well, for instance, she only ever gives them cold food.'

'Cold food? Salads? Cold meals?'

'No. I mean she only cooks once a week and then just goes on serving it out. Cold. Potatoes, cabbage, meat. All cold. You can heat it up yourself if you like, but *she* don't do it. Now that's not normal, is it?'

'No,' said Joan. 'I suppose she had a reason for it, though?'

'Yes. She said it gave her more time for other things. So it did. But one thing leads to another, and what with never sitting down to a meal together and always queueing up to warm our food at the cooker, well we never spoke to each other. No one ever really had a conversation in that house. When you get outside and look back, you think, that's not the way to live.'

'No,' said Joan Eames, and made a note to tell her boss that Check Colver's life *might* have produced the pressures out of which a murder could come.

There was one point where these paths could have crossed.

Sheila Daly and her husband had been in the news once before. *That* time it had been the husband's fault. On Thursday, April 28, 196—, he had been found dead in the garage of the house they had shared in Pestalozzi Street. Eight days later, on Friday, May 6, the inquest on him had been held. The Coroner took the evidence. Philip Daly had been known to be depressed. He had lost his job. (He was an actor of sorts.) He was using up his savings. His wife had taken a job and he had told a neighbour he hated her having to support him. He was the same age as his wife, but had looked younger. Everyone said so, someone even said so at the inquest, and the photograph that appeared in the papers at the time showed that it was so. He looked boyish, a lad.

'He was a very bright boy usually,' said the last person to whom he had spoken, a neighbouring housewife, who was giving evidence before the Coroner. 'As cheerful as could be when things were going well, but when he was down he was very down.'

'Yes, he was unhappy,' agreed his wife, when her turn came. 'I couldn't seem to shift his mood.'

So it was easily established that he had been depressed. However, he had not left a note before he shut himself in the garage and started the engine of the car and waited for the carbon monoxide to work. It was a small garage and the doctor reckoned that the air would have become poisoned within five minutes, give or take a minute or two. In the absence of a note it was difficult to be sure exactly what motive had impelled him to suicide.

'Did he ever threaten to kill himself?' the Coroner had asked his wife.

'No,' Sheila had answered. 'Not to me.'

'And you have no idea why he might have done it?'

Those in court, not many, it was hardly a cause célèbre, thought Sheila hesitated perceptibly, then she said: 'No.'

'The person who had found Philip Daly was the boy delivering an evening paper. He delivered it at five o'clock after finishing school. The way in which he found the body was in itself not without interest. He was a fourteen-year-old boy due to leave school within the next six months. He already had his job lined up, he was going to work with a veterinarian, and if he liked it and his father could raise the money, he was going to train as one himself. He was a boy who liked animals. The Dalys had a large black and white cat with whom he was already friendly. When he saw this cat asleep on the high window ledge of the garage, he approached it to speak to it. Then, through the glass he decided the cat was dead, not asleep. He went to tell someone . . . And so Philip Daly was discovered.

It was because of the cat and the feeling that Daly would

not have killed himself without removing the cat from the garage first that some people thought he could not have committed suicide.

A verdict of suicide was, however, returned.

The evening paper had only been delivered by the boy who found the body for the last week. Previously the round had been in the hands of another boy, who had now left to take up a full-time job with a firm of decorators. That boy was Charles Colver.

So Charles Colver could have known Sheila Daly. Their paths had crossed. And he could have known exactly what she looked like and how attractive she was.

They were still looking for Martin Kelly, but they hadn't managed to find him yet. He wasn't in his office and he wasn't to be found at home.

That was Saturday, the eighth day. Later that night, someone went into the old graveyard and tore up the grass on some of the graves and trampled it around and smeared mud on one of the stones.

When Isaiah Steinberg and his wife left Dresden, in Saxony, they were following their people's history. Centuries ago, in a wave of religious zeal, their Khazar forebears had been converted to Judaism. They had never seen the shores of Galilee, but henceforth they were Jews. But when they left Germany it was not only on a retreat from the life of the ghetto and the pogrom (Dresden had both), but for other reasons. Isaiah Steinberg was a reader and a thinker, he hated authoritarian government and believed in freedom and the political responsibility of the ordinary working man. As a lad he had been excited by the French Revolution and then had watched the career of Napoleon Bonaparte with frustration and despair. He thought of emigrating to the newly formed United States of America, but his resources were limited and his wife was pregnant with her fourth child. 'We shall go to England,' he said. 'There we shall be both free and I shall be a voter. Jacob Spitzer has told me so.' He was over optimistic and mis-informed. In 1815 there was no vote for people like Isaiah

Steinberg. It was not until 1830 that the first Jewish eman-
cipation bill was brought in, and this the Steinbergs did
not live to see.

The family settled in London, south of the bridges in a
newly built area, where the brick of the houses was still
yellow and ungrimed. Isaiah Steinberg rented the house in
Great Barnabas Street for £12 a year. The top floor he let
rented. Isaiah was a good landlord and liked to know his
tenants. In the five years he lived in the house he had two
tenants. The first was a widow called Jennings who soon
moved to another town; the second was a medical student
called Parkinson. Parkinson was also a keen theologian.
He took his landlord to St. Barnabas Church, the incum-
bent of which was an intense Hell-Fire Evangelical called
Wilberforce. Something in his eloquence called to that
spirit in Steinberg which had moved his Khazar ancestors,
and Isaiah responded with an ardour which surprised him.
He heard the Word and was converted. His friend Parkinson watched him with increasing apprehension; he was
becoming interested in nervous diseases, and thought he
saw symptoms in his landlord.

The district in those days was a rowdy, crowded world
with sedate family houses like the one the Steinbergs
inhabited fronting older slums. Early in 1820 there was an
election in the constituency. Parkinson watched as Steinberg's excitement grew higher and higher. He noticed the
ominous patches of red on the man's cheeks which faded
and rose as he talked, like the stigmata of a disease. Two
candidates were contesting the seats, one a Tory, the other
an out and out radical called John Leach. The franchise
was not universal in 1820, far from it, but this borough
had a fair number of electors all keen to use, and sell, their
votes. The hustings were lively. Isaiah was always present
and he very often took his family: his silent wife, his lively
son who already spoke cheerful Cockney, and his beautiful
eldest daughter.

'I shall support Leach,' said Isaiah enthusiastically. He
had no vote to use, his support was entirely moral and
vocal; still, that counted for something to a man like John
Leach who must look for support where he could. 'He is

for universal suffrage. In five years I shall be a citizen of Great Britain and a voting man.'

'I shouldn't believe all Leach tells you,' observed Parkinson mildly.

'You only say that because you are a Tory.'

'I'm not a Tory, in fact.'

'He is an honest man.'

'Oh yes, of course.'

'He believes in universal suffrage. Every man should vote. He even believes that women should come to it. In time.'

'Oh really!' said the young doctor. 'The brain of a woman is several ounces lighter than that of a man. As an anatomist, I tell you that. Vote, indeed.'

'I tell you, you should talk to Leach. He would convince you. All women need is education, you know. He is to advise me about Rebecca. For my wife it is too late, alas.'

'You know his reputation, of course?' said Parkinson hesitantly.

'What reputation?'

'He is a man of great gallantries.'

'My wife is a woman above reproach, sir,' said Steinberg, the colour in his cheeks coming and going even faster than usual.

'Oh yes, I was not suggesting,' began the flustered Parkinson.

'And my daughter is fourteen. Fourteen!'

'Ah yes, indeed,' said Parkinson, and fell silent. Secretly he wanted to feel his friend's pulse and to test the perspiration on the skin.

'Mr. Leach is my friend and visits my house,' said Steinberg with dignity.

'Oh well, perhaps it was debts I heard people talking about and not . . .' He saw a strange expression cross his friend's face. 'You haven't lent him money?'

'I have *given* a little to a noble cause,' said Steinberg. 'A very little.'

You haven't much to give, thought Parkinson. But you're noble yourself. Yes, I do believe you are. He began to wonder on the boundary between nobility and madness and where they touched and when one became the other. 'Does your head ache?'

'Ache? No, no,' said Steinberg. 'You doctors are always looking for illness.'

Parkinson shook his head. Slowly he went upstairs to the top floor he had furnished and occupied.

'Come to the hustings on Election night,' his friend called up after him.

A platform with banners and decorative draperies had been set up for the Radical candidate outside the Blue Anchor public house. The rival faction said that John Leach spent too much time inside the Blue Anchor, but the Radicals affirmed that this was just jealousy as *their* candidate was incomparably better looking and more of a man than the Tory, whom they called 'Sandy Tom'. He was a tall, thin, red-haired barrister called Thomas de Tombs Sands, and he was built to be caricatured by Phiz. Even his nose seemed to have that extra twist at the end the artist admired, and provided even if nature hadn't. Sands had a wife called Lady Elizabeth, a square soldierly lady and three sandy-haired little girls. The little girls were exact miniatures of their father. Gossip said that there ought to have been plenty of miniatures of John Leach walking around the district if nature had had its way, but he was reputed to know lots of precautionary 'French tricks'. Election gossip of the district was both bawdy and libellous. The London working man was not mealy mouthed, and if he had been, John Leach was not the man to inspire gentility. He was a good rousing orator and made noisy speeches. His rival spoke in a quietly laboured tone and John Leach's supporters said that Lady Elizabeth would have made better speeches. 'Three cheers for the Tory's lady,' they called in a ribald way, 'and may she and her 'usband never find out she's the better man o' the two of 'em.'

On Election night John Leach had all the shouts but his rival had all the votes; so in the end 'Sandy Tom' and his lady had the best of it.

The streets stayed crowded with citizens celebrating the Election. Some hours later, Parkinson, standing at the edge of the pushing, shouting and fighting (although in a good-humoured boisterous way) crowd saw two men asking for John Leach. They were not educated men, but certainly had an air of authority about them. He stopped one and asked him what he wanted.

The man touched his hat, seeing he had to deal with gentry. 'Just a little matter of debt, sir,' he said quietly. 'Waiting to see what way the Election went. An M.P. can't be touched for debt, sir.'

'So I know. You and your companion are sheriff's officers?'

'That's right, sir. Just doing our duty. It's the Fleet now for Mr. Leach.'

The Fleet was London's notorious debtor prison. It was old and crowded and full of rotting humanity: it was easier to get into it than out.

'D'ye know where Mr. Leach is to be found, sir?' said the man, giving Parkinson a keen look. He was not unpractised in his trade.

Silently Parkinson shook his head, although he thought he could have guessed, and began to walk home. Through the crowded streets behind him padded the two Sheriff's officers. A few yards from the house Parkinson overtook his landlord, also going home. He was carrying a small jug of gin in his hand, although he did not drink.

'Got old Leach back home, have you then?'

'I am proud to offer Mr. Leach a little hospitality,' said Steinberg stiffly. He looked tired.

'I thought you had. There's someone looking for him.'

'Many will look for a man of prominence like Mr. Leach.'

'This is someone whom he'd rather not see, I fancy. Take my word for it and give him the hint.'

'I do not understand you,' said Steinberg, walking more slowly.

'Just tell him the tipstaff's after him and he'll understand fast enough.' He added, 'And I should tell him quickly if I were you.' He had sensitive ears and had heard the double tread behind him.

Steinberg went into the house just ahead of his lodger.

There was the original narrow hallway (at some later date going to be knocked down) but you were in the main sitting room almost before you knew it. He was close enough to Steinberg to hear his sudden indrawn breath and see the deep colour blotch his neck and throat. Then Steinberg rushed forward.

John Leach was sprawled in the big armchair, drunken and laughing, and on his lap with his hand in her skirts was the young Steinberg girl. She was crying and giggling at the same time. John Leach was feeding her gin from an old cup. When he saw them at the door he made a half-hearted attempt to get up, then sank back in the chair.

Steinberg grabbed his daughter and slapped her face. She staggered from the blow and Parkinson caught her in his arms. He placed her in another chair and rushed over to grab Steinberg who had Leach by the throat. 'I'll kill him, I'll kill him,' he was saying.

Steinberg was heavy and strong, but Parkinson had learned a trick or two in the hospital wards and slowly he levered the hands free.

'I'll kill them both,' said Steinberg.

'Quiet,' said Parkinson. Leach sagged in the chair, but he was breathing. Parkinson moved his body between the two men without letting go of his hold on his landlord. 'Kill, kill,' muttered Steinberg.

There was a heavy rap on the door and the tipstaff and his assistant stood there. 'Now, what's this?'

'Nothing,' said Parkinson. 'Nothing much.'

'Don't look like it, sir, if I may say so,' said the tipstaff, gazing round the room. 'And there's Mr. Leach. Up to your old games, are you? Mr. Leach and I are old friends.'

Leach swore.

'Such language. How is a poor man like me ever to better himself if a gentleman like you talks like that? Who's to teach me? Come on now, I'm waiting.'

'I won't be in the Fleet long,' said Leach thickly.

'We'll see, sir, shall we? Come along now.' He put a hand under Leach and so did his assistant. He winked at Parkinson. 'Your gentleman's gone quiet,' he said.

'Yes.' Parkinson looked down at Isaiah Steinberg with

anxiety. The man, his violence gone, had sunk on to the floor and was moaning softly.

'Anything wrong with him, is there? Is he hurt?'

'Only in his heart,' said Parkinson.

When the house was quiet again and the frightened Steinberg women, wife, mother and daughters, all four, peaceably together with the eldest son in the back parlour, Parkinson went to look at his landlord now lying in bed. He appeared to be asleep and the young man crept out. Then to refresh himself and please the lad, he took the youngest Steinberg boy, whom he was teaching Latin, out for a walk along the river as far as the bridge. The night was clear and the stars bright; they pointed out the pattern of the Plough to each other as they walked. The boy was a clever lad.

And it was while they were out that Isaiah Steinberg stole down from his bedroom and killed all of his family in the house, so that only this one boy remained of his seed.

10

The desecration of the graveyard added an element of superstition and nastiness to the murder. You never had to dig very deep round here to discover both these elements, as John Coffin very well knew. They existed side by side with genuine charity and kindness. He had long ago given up trying either to condemn or to justify the inhabitants of his manor. In spite of the air of bustling earthiness the district liked to put on, underneath it had always provided a rich soil for strange obsessions. 'We have more nuts per square mile than any other manor in London,' Coffin said. 'We're a focus for them. Who has the Flying Saucer experts? We do. Who has the man who sleeps every night in a magic circle so the vampire bat won't get him? We do. *And* he's the manager of a local Friendly Society by day. Who has their M.P. murdered? We do.'

In fact they had a high incidence of violent crime in their neighbourhood and he knew it. While he was worrying about the murder of Thomas Barr and Sheila Daly he was also wondering what the focus for this violence was. The spoiling of the graveyard was just one more manifestation of what he had to face every day.

Another manifestation, although one he was not yet very well aware of, was taking place in the house of John Plowman, P.N.A.F.H. He had his name and these initials painted in white on a black board. No brass plate for him. Brass was too permanent. Tomorrow he might be something different.

Mark Berkeley entered John Plowman's waiting room, saw no one was waiting, and went straight through into what John now called his surgery. This was also the family sitting room. But it had a large roll top desk with a stiff chair for John and a softer one for the patient.

'Have a look at my arm, John,' said Mark. 'Giving me trouble again.'

John, who was sitting at the desk, put on a pair of large blue-tinted spectacles which made him look like a newly arrived Martian. 'You should have knocked,' he said.

'I did knock. You didn't hear.'

'You did not knock,' said John severely. 'You forget I have paranormal cognition of events. Always have had. I know what you do.'

'Have a look at my arm then,' said Mark. 'It's giving me gyp.'

'I don't have to look,' said John, turning to look at a paper on his desk. 'I know what the trouble is. Pain radiating from the left shoulder down to the elbow.'

'You saw the way I held it.'

'If you have no faith you need not come to me,' said John Plowman.

'I have faith,' said Mark. 'You did me a lot of good with my back.'

'Very well.' John got up and put his hands just over Mark's left arm near the shoulder, not touching him, but rather as if he was blessing him. 'Ah yes, very hot here. I can feel it.' Now he ran his hands gently over the shoulder. 'Take your coat off. Thanks. Ah, here we are. Strong psychic lesion here. It's not coming from your shoulder, you know.'

'It's not? That's where the pain is.'

'No. It's coming from the neck. Maybe even higher up and at the base of the skull.' He was feeling underneath the greying hair. 'Got anything on your mind? That could be it.'

'You're supposed to tell me.'

'Oh no. There has to be a flow between us,' said John. 'You've got a block.' He withdrew his hand. 'Yes, this is going to take a long time. Yes, I feel a very strong block in your mind.' He clasped his hands together for a moment, then unclasping them laid them on Mark's shoulder. 'I may be able to give you some temporary help. There . . . I can do no more than alleviate at the moment. How's that?'

Mark moved his shoulder experimentally. 'Feels easier.'

'Good.' John consulted a big diary. 'You can have another appointment a week today,' he said in a business-like manner.

'Oh, thank you . . . You did me a tremendous lot of good before.' He put his hand into a pocket and drew out a wallet.

John Plowman held up a hand. 'You know I cannot accept payment.' He watched alertly as the wallet stayed still. 'There's a big dish in the hall as you go out if you want to help our cause.'

'How *is* business?'

'Not bad. A full surgery last night. It varies. But I'm building up some loyalties. Bound to be a bit slow at first. I'm getting known a bit. Yes, I think I can say that.'

'You always have been known round here, haven't you?'

In his time John Plowman had founded a Temple of Heavenly Love, organised a club for watching Unidentified Flying Objects, and sponsored one or two visitors from Outer Space. He was indeed known for his esoteric interests.

'It was all preparation,' he answered. 'I see now that all my other activities have led me to what I am now. Always I believed in what I did. Now I am no longer testing. This is *real*.'

Mark placed his contribution in the dish by the door. It was a polished wooden bowl of some dark wood that looked as though it might have been a salad bowl in the Plowman household.

John put his hand on Mark's shoulder. 'Old friend, I know I can help you,' he said. 'The gods be with you.' He was obliged in his trade not to be too specific about any particular deity. Zeus or Jehovah, he was on nodding terms with them both.

'He's not such an old friend,' said his wife from the kitchen door. She was watching John with an enigmatic expression. They had been married for thirty years but he still didn't know all she thought about things.

'I have known him on and off for a long time,' he said.

'And we're neighbours.' He frowned. 'He looks sick. Don't you think so?'

'Yes,' observed his wife briefly.

'I think I can help him. I really feel I can. With your help, of course.' His wife was a qualified nurse. 'I think it gives me confidence to have you here.'

'Yes, I see you don't go far wrong,' she said. Again ambiguously, he reflected.

'That's right, dear,' he answered. 'But you seem a little uneasy yourself. What is troubling you?'

Silently she moved round the room, dusting here, replacing some papers here. All totally unnecessary work, he realised, and indulged in to cover up her feelings. She must be thinking something out. Although at various times he had practised precognition, attempted telepathy and had a go at telemetry, he had never really had much of a line on his wife.

'You heard about the graveyard being messed up?' she said suddenly.

'Yes. Nasty. I thought of going round there and offering a silent stream of prayer to counteract it.'

His wife looked thoughtful. 'Don't. Just leave it.'

'Do you know something, dear?' he asked. Although she did not have the advantages of telepathy and precognition like him, she frequently knew things he did not.

'Well, it's rather strange,' she said, still fidgeting round. 'You know I took up planchette again, when we got back.' Recently, the Plowmans had been away from the district, living in an anonymous way in another suburb. This vacation, if you could call it that, had many of the unexplained aspects that attended so many of their activities. To John Coffin and his colleagues it had looked like a retreat from a nasty situation in which they had been involved; an earlier series of murders in his manor.

'Yes, I was glad to see you get back to that.'

'I've never had any gift for it. Anyone can get some sort of result, of course.'

'You underrate yourself, my dear.'

She ignored this. 'But I've been having sessions lately with Mrs. Idwall. She's really talented. She was on the stage for a time, of course.' It was asides such as this that threw her husband; he never knew what to make of them. 'She gets something interesting nine times out of ten.'

'Clever girl.'

'She has a good control. A girl called Celestial Joy. She's from the Orient.'

'They're so often foreigners,' said her husband.

'Her ideas on life are a little Oriental too, especially on marriage. But that's understandable when you consider that Mrs. Idwall's first husband was from Japan.'

'Was he?'

'Oh yes, a very little man, Nippo, they used to call him. On the stage he was, in a juggling act. That's where Deirdre met him.'

'What happened to him?'

'Passed over,' said Mrs. Plowman briefly. 'We think he's really the one behind Celestial Joy. But he hasn't come right out and said so. Lying low. We think he may be married to her.'

'There is no marrying or giving in marriage behind the Barrier,' said John, shocked.

'From what she knows they ought to be married,' said Mrs. Plowman, who sometimes showed tenacious traces of her Methodist upbringing, in spite of the diversity of her experiences since then. 'However,' and she paused, 'we had a session last night.'

'I thought you were occupied,' said her husband. 'I didn't go into your little sanctum.'

'You were having your surgery. Rather sparse last night, weren't you?'

'We shall build up.'

'Yes.' She turned to her husband and he saw that she was really troubled. 'Last night we kept having interruptions. Another person kept pushing past Celestial Joy and making comments.' She clasped her hands.

'Tell me what,' he commanded.

'Nothing very coherent. A sort of matter. Rather disturbing, though. There seemed to be some sort of murderer trying to get through.'

They stared at each other.

'Did he say who he was?' asked John Plowman.

She shook her head. 'A man, though. Celestial Joy couldn't identify him. She said he seemed to be a sort of paper man.'

'No message?'

'Nothing I could understand.'

'One often doesn't see at the time,' said John Plowman.

'I just got the impression there was someone there struggling to get out to us . . .'

'Oh, how nasty,' said John Plowman spontaneously.

'The grave that was disturbing belongs to Old Steinberg,' said his wife. 'He was a murderer . . . I just wondered if it was him, trying, somehow or other, to get through.' She looked at him. 'It's all mixed up, isn't it?'

She told her husband and later he told one of his friends and the friend told his wife. In this manner it escaped into the gossip of the neighbourhood. Naturally no one quite believed it, but it was handed round as a sort of flesh creeper, a variant on the Dracula theme. A horror film of this sort was running in the neighbourhood cinema at the moment. Quite a few people said this was where Mrs. Plowman had got the idea. It was a fact, however, that the grave had been disturbed.

Other rumours were going around too, of course. But these mainly concerned the last hours in the life of Thomas Barr and Sheila, his secretary. The rumours ranged from the relatively mild, to the effect that he and Sheila had a good friendship going but nothing more, to those which concluded that more than business was transacted in the house in Great Barnabas Street.

Some of these stories got through to Camilla Barr (who anyway was sophisticated and worldly enough to have invented them herself). All of them got through to John Coffin who was still trying to find what had really happened in those last hours when Thomas Barr was alive and dead.

11

He could have taken his study back beyond the day of
death to the very day of Tom's birth in Shropshire over
thirty-six years ago. But both his parents were dead and
had been dead for many years. He could have taken his
study back to schooldays, to University, back to the beginning of his interest in political things. But you have to
start somewhere, and so he decided to start with his marriage, because marriage is so often the start of something.

He had married Camilla not long after becoming an
M.P. He had got into Parliament in a by-election in 1962
and been returned with an increased majority at the Gen-
eral Election of 1964. He was safe, everyone said, to get
back in again as long as he wanted. Everyone non-political,
that is. If you were political then you said either gloomily
or happily, according to your party, that the position was
doubtful. But with people who didn't care whether they
had a vote or not, he was popular because he was good
looking and appeared at plenty of local functions. He also
did a good deal of hard work about housing, schools, and
hospitals in his constituency, as well as listening to the
worries and grievances of those who came into his Friday
evening surgery.

'Tom was a hard worker. A good boy,' said his agent,
Fred Dick. 'Of course, he had to be careful where he put
his feet, you have to be in a constituency like this.'

'What's wrong with it,' said Coffin, who was questioning him.

Fred Dick scratched his head. 'Extremes there, you
know. Communists down by the docks. Old Labour that
row of semi's down by the railway. Still loyal but dying

out. Then there's all the big new blocks of flats—trouble there is to get them to the polls at all, and when you do they vote for the name they heard of last. Then there's the new smart streets, all well off—New Left.' He shrugged. 'I reckon some of them sneak off and vote for another party when they think of their taxes. But you can't rely on form these days the way you used to be able to. Voters do anything they fancy now, no loyalty at all.'

'Really?' said Coffin, interested to get this run down on a district he saw from quite another angle. Now, if asked he would have said that down by the docks the commonest crimes involved money and the main incentive was a quick profit. Sometimes it would be an amateur job, and sometimes there would be a tie-in with a professional gang, but money was the motive.

In the big blocks of flats you got crimes of personal violence. Slashing, molesting, rape and murder. Suicides, too, were frequent, although no longer a crime. In the smart slick streets so newly risen in the world it was usually the foreign 'au pair girl' who was in trouble. Or else a house was broken into and its valuables rapidly transported. The first mink coat ever to be stolen in his area was stolen from one of these workmen's cottages turned into a smart town house. They seemed more sinned against than sinning in such houses, but you could never tell.

Murder however could appear anywhere. Even in those stolid little streets which solemnly voted Labour and ran up no debts. As a matter of fact, the very nastiest murder he had ever faced had happened behind one of those grey brick walls. A girl had been cut up and sewed into a sack . . . the murder was still unsolved. The house had been empty at the time, the inhabitants, an aged couple were on holiday. When it happened it was proved they knew nothing of the girl or her murder. They had a nephew though, a petty officer in the Navy, with a wife and three children, and up for promotion. The girl had been coloured and pregnant. But nothing had ever been proved. It was part of life as lived in Coffin's manor.

'All the same, I think Tom would have had a clear run home provided he kept his nose clean.'

'Any reason to think he hadn't?'

'Well, you know how these things are. No one's fault.'

'No?'

'I wonder you don't know about it. Probably you do really and are just testing me out to see how far I'll go.'

'And how far will you go?'

'Now that's not fair. Still, when his secretary's husband killed himself, there was a lot of talk. She'd only just started to work for Tom, but that didn't stop people blaming him, saying there was something between the two of them that threw the husband off his balance. Nonsense, of course.'

'Was it nonsense?'

'There may have been something,' he said, after a pause. 'To tell you the truth, I've never been quite sure.'

After the inquest on her husband was when the talk had really started. He had apparently killed himself. But what had driven him to it? Sheila said she didn't know. Her neighbours thought she might have had some idea. Her husband had hated the idea of her going to work. From there it was an easy staircase of ideas and they made it in one great leap.

'It was a funny business. Know what I mean? I couldn't see through it from one end to the other. But can you ever? The more I know of people the less clear I am about them. There's always that little odd thing extra, isn't there?'

'What did he say?'

'I never raised it with Tom.'

'You never had it out with him?' asked Coffin, as if he couldn't believe it. He lived in a world where you came right out and asked things.

'There was a devaluation crisis on at that time. That dates it a bit, doesn't it? The talk seemed to die down. I did nothing about it. Tom wasn't an easy man.'

'Was his wife with him then?'

'She'd already gone to New York. That was a funny business. They seemed happy enough. I'm sure *he* was. And then suddenly off she goes. All perfectly friendly, but she didn't come back.'

'I don't think you're being quite straight with me.'

'Yes, I am. Perfectly straight. I know nothing I haven't told you. Or next to nothing. Nothing of importance, that is.'

'Tell me what wasn't important then.'

'I went in once when Sheila was taking a telephone call. Nothing in that, of course, she was the man's secretary. But it was a personal call. I'm sure of that. And from the look on her face, I'd say she hated it. Either that or she was frightened. I wondered if someone had been threatening her.'

'When was this?'

'About fifteen days ago. And then once again, a week later.'

'I like your nothing,' said Coffin. 'I like it very much.'

'There was something between them, Tom and the girl Sheila,' Fred Dick said. 'Some sort of extra relationship. I admit I felt it, working in the same room with them so often I was bound to. But whatever it was, it wasn't what you think.'

'Did his wife know?'

'She was certainly trying to,' said Fred. 'She was employing a detective, Martin Kelly.'

'How do you know that?'

'It pays me to know that sort of thing. I went to call on him myself. He was rude.'

'He often is.'

Fred grinned. 'Well, I asked a few rude questions. Don't hold it against him.'

'You don't know why Mrs. Barr sent for him? Or how she got hold of his name?'

'No.' He shook his head. 'She could have had a letter. Or a telephone call. I'd favour a telephone call myself. Like Sheila had, probably.'

'A telephone call all the way to New York?' said Coffin.

'Why not?'

Their eyes met. 'Yes, why not,' said Coffin. 'I could probably run a check on her New York number. Might even trace one back.'

'And even if you don't get anywhere, you'll know something about the person who made that call.'

Coffin looked at him silently.

'Work it out for yourself. Not everyone would make such a call. I think it tells you something about class, education and income. Even in these days you have to be up in a certain bracket to think of making a transatlantic call. A labourer down at the docks wouldn't do it.'

'You seem pretty convinced about the existence of that call. Are you sure you're just guessing?'

Their eyes met.

'I had a call myself,' admitted Fred. 'Just a voice. And it said: Watch your boss. He's up to tricks.'

'Would you recognise the voice?'

Fred shook his head silently.

'And did you believe it?'

'Belief, disbelief, I didn't try for either. If I thought about it at all I thought someone was out to get Tom Barr. I wiped it out of my mind.'

'You didn't. Nor could his wife if she got something like that.' Coffin made a note on a pad in front of him. He cleared his throat. 'Now I have to ask this. Could there be a political motive?'

'We've never gone in for assassination in this country.'

'But could the motive have arisen from anything in Thomas Barr's life as a politician?'

'You can't separate public and private life. Especially with men like Tom. He was all politician. Perhaps that's what Camilla couldn't take. In that sense, yes, his killing could have arisen out of politics. Yes, I do believe that it was because Tom was a public figure that he died the way he did.' Fred Dick looked wryly at Coffin. 'I'm being honest with you, but perhaps not helpful.'

'I think you've been helpful,' said Coffin.

He went back to his own office and set in train the check on calls received at Camilla Barr's New York apartment. His experience of his American colleagues was that they were methodical and helpful and would trace the call if anyone could.

The file on Charles Colver was lying on his desk when he got back. He put it to one side. If there had been a telephone call to Camilla Barr and if the caller was later the killer of her husband and his secretary, then Charles Colver, interesting though he was as a side line, was out as the murderer. He wasn't the one to have been making a telephone call to New York. Class wise, he didn't fit. It was always nice to know the social position of your murderer.

The last days of Thomas Barr's life, as the police disinterred it, seemed unpromisingly normal. He had attended to his political duties, he had put in a brief appearance at the offices of the newspaper for which he did occasional work and which retained him as an adviser on economic affairs. In the afternoon there was a gap when no one seemed to have seen him, but before this he had taken a party of constituents round the House and later had lunch with the leader of the group.

Coffin had a talk with this man on his way home. He lived in the neighbourhood, just round the corner from Coffin himself. He knew him as the man who kept the donkey. This was an aged grey beast rescued, so gossip had it, from the knacker's yard by its present owner, whom it repaid with steady indifference. The children of all the surrounding districts loved it. It ignored them too. The man was called March.

'How's the donkey?' Coffin asked, by way of a beginning.

'Fine. You don't want to buy him, do you? We have to keep him in a stable across the park and it costs a fortune. Surly brute, too. Honestly, I often feel like sending him back over to the dog meat factory again. After all, dogs are human too, aren't they?'

'I didn't come about the donkey.'

'No.' He fell silent. 'No, I never supposed it was that really. Except it's that old donkey we all keep inside us and which gets outside sometimes. That's what you came and asked about? The donkey inside Tom Barr. Have a drink anyway.'

'Was there a donkey inside Thomas Barr?'

March made the drink strong and took a long draught. 'Yes. A great big genuine donk, jumbo sized. Drink up.'

He took another long drink himself. 'Yes, that was old Tom.'

'Could you make that more explicit?'

'After another drink like this one I could be much more explicit. Much more. For a clever man, Tom couldn't keep out of trouble. Perhaps he'd see it coming but he never got out of the way in time. My old donkey's like that. I am myself sometimes, so are you, I bet.' He squinted at Coffin across the glass. 'But Tom was like it *all* the time. He did everything the hard way. Take Camilla now. If ever an M.P. needed a wife that was good and loyal and by his side, Tom did. But he was going to have to work at it. Camilla wasn't easy. Yet she was very tied up with him when they married.'

'She loved him?'

'Yes,' said March doubtfully. 'Whatever that means. Let me at least say she was excessively interested in him.'

'But she went away all the same.'

'Well, I never asked either of them the reason for that. But they did quarrel. From quite early on. Camilla had a quick temper and Tom had a slow one and never the twain shall meet.'

'So what went wrong?'

'I suppoes really Camilla didn't like being just Tom's *subsidiary*, that was what it must have felt like, and Tom, although he surely didn't mean the rot to set in, couldn't stop it.'

'I suppose if you care enough you stop it happening,' said Coffin, half to himself.

'Don't you believe it,' said March, freshening up his drink. 'Either you're born with your feet walking in the right direction or you're not. But don't let's get on to theology. Ever read Teilhard de Chardin? A very interesting man.'

'No theology,' said the policeman.

March smiled, drank and went on.

'Even his secretary came in for some of it with Tom. When she started work for him she was a happily married woman, then within a few months her husband is dead, and within two years she's dead herself, bought it herself with Tom. Watch the company you keep, that's what I say.'

'You felt there was trouble coming?'

'We all felt there was trouble coming.' He put his glass down on the table and looked sober and unhappy. 'There was talk. Tom Barr and Sheila Daly are having it off all the time in office hours. I don't know where the talk started, or who was pushing it out. But it was there. Even my wife knew it, and honestly what with the kids and the donk she never knows anything.' He hesitated. 'I did wonder if she'd passed it on to Camilla, they used to be good friends, but she swears she didn't. Still, Camilla knew.'

'How much truth was there in it?'

March merely shrugged.

'Did you ever raise it with Tom Barr?'

'Yes, once.' He added, 'Over lunch, the last time we met. The last day he was alive.'

'What did he say?'

'He was surprised.'

'So you think there was nothing in the gossip?'

'No, it just means he was surprised. I think it was real surprise, but I don't know. I'll tell you one thing about Tom that day though; he was tired. Bone tired.'

He turned his glass upside down on the table and stared at it.

'I wish I knew what happened to Tom. And why. And how.' He turned to Coffin in a puzzled way. 'I tell you, I just can't visualise anything.'

His own house was empty when Coffin got back to it. His wife and child were away. Carefully he removed from the refrigerator the pre-cooked meal wrapped in tin foil with the words 'Day Two' marked on it and put it in the oven. This was 'Day Three' but he hadn't been eating at home much lately. He wondered what it was. As the heat got through, it began to smell like curry. Curry, they said, improved with keeping.

The curry was hot and full of flavour, but the rice, having been too long in the freezer, was wet and powdery.

Like much in Coffin's experience, he'd got the good and
the bad in about equal quantities. He was used to it, and,
in a masochistic kind of way, enjoyed it.

Coffee he made himself. It was a task to which he had,
over the years, brought practised skill. He got the water
very hot, boiling if he could remember, then he put two
spoonfuls of powdered coffee in a cup and stirred it. Then
he let it get cold before he drank it.

He was stirring it when the telephone rang. It was
Inspector Dove.

'I think I know where Thomas Barr was in that gap in
the afternoon.'

'Where was he then?'

'He took a taxi and he went home.'

'He did?'

'Yes, and he kept the taxi waiting, and then he came back
and gave the taxi driver an address in Magellan Street.'

'Magellan Street? But that's where . . .'

'Yes, that's where Martin Kelly has his office. And that's
where Thomas Barr, M.P. went. To call on the detective
who was probably watching him on behalf of his wife.'

'How long was he there? Is it known?'

'Not so far. Nor do we know if he actually saw Kelly.'

'And then he went back to the House of Commons?'

'Yes.' There was a strange note in Dove's voice.

'Go on,' said Coffin. 'You've got more to come.'

'Yes. He went to the Library there. They have a Law
Library, you know.'

'I didn't know.'

'Well, they do have. Members pop in and out, looking
things up. Tom Barr used it sometimes. He used it the
day he died. He went and spent some time studying the
law report of the trial of Isaiah Steinberg for murder. He
also had some contemporary newspapers—the *Times* and
the *Morning Post*—out to study.'

'So he was interested in old Steinberg?'

'You know what?' said Dove. 'I think he knew something was coming.'

'Yes,' said Coffin. 'I think he knew. I think Sheila Daly
knew. I think they both saw it coming.'

'Something else,' said Dove. 'Just a coincidence, I suppose.' He paused.

'Yes?' prompted Coffin.

'The man I sent down to the House of Commons is an intelligent chap. Knows his way about books. That's why I sent him. And he took it into his head to go down to the British Museum Library and see what they had there on Isaiah Steinberg.' He paused again.

'And so?'

'And so he discovered that a few days before him someone had had out the relevant books on Steinberg. Unused for sixty years those books had been, and now they start moving.

'And who was reading them?'

'Not just anyone can read in the British Museum Library. You have to apply for a ticket. So whoever ordered the books must have done this. But on the order slip the name is scrawled in such a way it's virtually illegible. It could be anything. The one thing that's clear is the date, also the seat number where he sat (if it was a he) B.32.'

'So we aren't so very much further advanced,' said Coffin. 'Unless we can find B.32, and that's not so likely. What about watching the seat?'

'B.32 seems to have finished with his pile of books. He hasn't been back to read again. They keep out books, you know, for a while, then return them to the stacks. B.32's books on Steinberg go back tomorrow. No, he won't be reading them again. I reckon he's got all he wants.'

'Someone must have been talking to Tom Barr about the Steinberg case and got him interested,' speculated Coffin. 'I wonder why?'

Down below he heard a taxi draw up, and then the sound of his wife's clear voice.

'Now I wonder why she's come home a day early?' He hated to look for a devious motive in his wife's behaviour, but he knew there often was one.

A small room in the Palace of Westminster, in that part of it called the House of Commons, was given over to the Prime Minister's secretaries. They had other rooms, of course, but this minute, relatively secluded room was used for meetings desired to be private. Naturally it was closely observed by everyone.

The three men arrived one after the other. They knew each other so well that no greeting was necessary. Nor was there need for any leading up to the subject which had brought them here.

'The P.M. wants a complete dossier on the Barr murder,' said the first man in. He had been sitting waiting.

'He has that already, Bob.'

'But not full enough.'

They both turned to look at the third man who had been the last arrival and was still panting a little.

'Hello Bob, hello Rupert.'

'Sit down and get your breath back,' said Rupert, pushing forward a chair. 'What kept you?'

'The Man himself.'

'Oh.' Both Robert Peters and Rupert Reeve absorbed the information with interest but it was Bob who went on speaking. 'Well, what does he say? You're closer to him than either of us are, Bruce.'

'He's mad.' Bruce took a deep breath. 'Yes, I've seen hornets in a better temper.'

'Your asthma's bad.'

'Just a little disturbance.'

'Yes, it was a pity Tom Barr got himself killed just now when he was going up in the world. He was getting the new ministry.'

'It wasn't announced,' said Bob. 'Not officially.'

'But everyone knows. There's been comment. And will be more. The Man's afraid they'll all say it's his bad judgement again.'

'Three by-elections coming up next month,' said Rupert, putting into speech what they all knew.

'And so it's got to be wrapped up and put away before then.'

'With a good whitewash job on Tom Barr.'

'No. No.' Bruce was thoughtful. 'Not necessarily; justice has to be seen to be done. Say what you like, in the end,

The Man is honest. No point now in being anything else. But if we know all the facts we can probably handle it.'

'If not?'

'If the by-elections go against us because of scandal, as they might, then the Government will be *out*,' said Bruce bluntly.

'I think we're all expecting that,' said Bob, his voice steady. He was an old campaigner and knew how to keep his nerve. 'But tomorrow is another day.' The truism contained all his philosophy.

'Bruce looks as though he doesn't see it that way,' observed Rupert.

'Oh, it's not just us, although that's bad enough. But it's a setback, don't you feel that? One more step downwards for us all. Disillusion, decadence—just words, but go on using them long enough and they get up and walk around. Democracy lives on confidence and that's just what's being drained away. I get the feeling someone's put the knife in.'

He sounded tired and depressed.

12

There was a telephone call for Coffin later that night. The caller, who had a friendly deep voice, said he was Robert Peters and left it at that. This may have been discretion, or confidence that Coffin knew him, and as a matter of fact, after a second's wild thought, Coffin did. He was one of the assistant secretaries in the Prime Minister's office.

'Like to have a talk with you, if you don't mind,' he said, in that confidential voice.

'Oh yes?'

'Lunch, perhaps? Tomorrow?'

'I can't spare time for lunch.'

'Oh, a drink then, before lunch?'

'Not even that.'

'Well, name your time then,' said Mr. Peters briefly. Coffin had the distinct impression there was some consultation going on off stage.

'Why don't *you* come and see me,' said Coffin, who knew what it was all about and knew he would have to go. He was just being difficult. No one ought to take me for granted, he thought.

'Ah yes, well, I don't think I could do that. You see, it's not just me. I won't be alone.'

You're telling me, thought Coffin. But I shall be. All alone and sticking my neck out. But he wanted to defend Tom Barr. He wanted very much to say that whatever happened it hadn't been Tom Barr's fault. It might not be true, but he wanted to say it.

'Could you make it convenient to meet me here at twelve noon?' said Mr. Peters.

'I'll be there,' said Coffin. As a matter of fact, he was

looking forward to going, and he would stay to lunch too. He hummed a little tune.

His wife looked at him sharply.

'I'm going to eat in a very important place,' he said.

'You mean you're going to eat it up. You love it.'

'That's about it,' he said happily.

'And what are you going to tell them?'

'I shall tell them that no, I do not yet know who killed Tom Barr, but that he probably knew he was going to be killed . . .'

'*Did* he?'

'Yes,' said Coffin, thinking of the fear-laden sweat on Thomas's chair.

'What else will you tell them?'

'I shall say: I don't know who killed him but a certain enquiry agent, a private detective, an ex-policeman is probably involved.'

'Martin Kelly?' exclaimed his wife.

'Yes. He was an old boy friend of yours once, wasn't he?'

'*No!* You've got so beastly since your illness.'

'Not more beastly. Just more open.'

His wife looked at him, baffled.

'And what will you say to them after that?' she asked, slightly mockingly. She did mock her husband when she got the chance, which lately wasn't often.

'If I'm honest, and even to them I might show a touch of honesty, then, if I'm honest, I'll say I've always believed there had to be a relationship between murderer and victim.'

'Like husband and wife, for instance?'

'Yes,' he said seriously. 'Or husband and lover or wife and lover, or all three. Or it could be mother and son. Or even just that the two met in a supermarket and hated each other. But I've always maintained there had to be a personal relationship somewhere. I've always said, you know, that at some stage murderer and victim have seen the whites of each other's eyes.' His face altered, becoming thinner, longer, angrier. 'But this could have been a *political* crime. It's got an impersonal feel to it, somehow.'

'Sounds *very* personal to me, all I've heard of it,' said his wife.

'No. It was degrading. Deliberate. An execution.'

'Are you going to say all that to them?'

'No. To them I shall just say I am investigating Camilla Barr and Martin Kelly.'

'They did know each other before she went to the States, you know,' said his wife.

'Who knew whom?'

'Camilla knew Martin Kelly. He was one of *you* then. I can remember the two of them at the Police New Year Ball. Tom and Camilla were guests of honour. She danced with Martin.'

'That doesn't mean anything,' said Coffin.

'No. I'm not saying it does. But she knew him. And he knew her.'

Martin Kelly rang Camilla's doorbell, pushing hard with his finger at the white button under the label 'Barr', then walking right in as soon as she opened the door.

'Oh, you're back,' she said.

'I was never away.' He looked round the room, which was empty except for the peke. 'I was just keeping out of the way while I thought things over.'

'Now you've done that?'

'Where did you get the dog?'

'He belongs to my cousin Jennifer. I told you about her.'

'That's right, you did.' Slowly he was relaxing his suspicions. 'Where is she now?'

'Out.'

'Not taking the dog?'

'She's out,' said Camilla patiently. 'She's gone to a party. Pekes don't like parties.'

'Don't try to be funny. There's nothing jokey in the situation you're in.'

Camilla looked at him silently.

'The police have been watching you.'

'Of course,' said Camilla. Her voice was as cold as her grey eyes.

'And they're coming round to thinking you've killed

your husband. They've been slower than me. I thought so quite early on. I think you could be a killer.'

'I've never killed anyone.'

'Wives don't need to do the killing themselves. They can get other people to do it for them. How did you fix it? Did you write letters? Make long impassioned pleas to him on the 'phone?'

'Him?' said Camilla.

'The killer,' said Martin Kelly. 'That poor devil. You had him on a string I expect. And you'd have been glad to have me there, too. I worked out your husband's movements and then you sent in your killer. Remote control. That's how you'd work it.'

'I didn't . . .' began Camilla. She was trembling. As she did so she just heard his voice say, 'Well, now I have a bargain to strike.'

'With me?'

'You come into it. But not with you alone. I'll let you know.'

Next morning, before going to Westminster, Coffin went round to Martin Kelly's office which was locked, shuttered and empty. The office was two small rooms in an old block. Below was a dealer in spices and herbs and above was a firm which called itself simply 'Importers (Continental) Ltd.'. Making a mental note to investigate this firm later, Coffin went downstairs and spoke to the woman who was polishing a brass plate inscribed 'Herbal Remedies & Co.'.

'Mr. Kelly around?' he said.

She shook her head silently.

'Seen him lately?'

Again she shook her head. Not a woman of many words, if action would do.

'This week? Last week?'

'Not seen him at all lately.' She gave the brass a rub with a grubby duster; she wasn't doing a very good job on it.

'Not working lately then, is he?'

'I dunno.'

She breathed on the brass and tried another rub. It looked no better. Worse, if anything.

'I think he comes in the evening,' she said suddenly, in a hoarse voice.

'Oh.' Coffin was interested. 'Why do you think that?'

'Just think so. Think he's been sleeping there. Comes in when it's quiet.'

It wasn't a bad idea, if Kelly wanted to hide. It was like the grave round here after office hours.

'You must have some reason for thinking that,' said Coffin.

She smiled slightly. 'Someone has to take the post in. No one else that I know of. Must be him.'

Coffin looked up the stairs. 'Think he's there now?' he asked.

She shook her head.

'Funny way to live,' said Coffin.

She smiled again, and he saw by the smile that she knew he was a policeman. 'He's not in debt,' she said. 'Don't think so.'

'No, not debt,' said Coffin.

Or, at any rate, not a debt of money, although there are other sorts. It meant that Kelly was either hiding from them, or from someone else, or from both.

'Well, thanks for telling me,' he said.

'I didn't tell you anything.'

'Something,' he said, smiling in his turn. 'Something.'

'I don't know what you came for,' she said, turning back to her brass.

'Just checking,' said Coffin. After all, if you're going to see the Prime Minister and say you're looking for a man but you don't know where he is, it's just as well to be sure you really don't. If you're uneasy, test that uneasiness and find out what it really amounts to. He knew now that his uneasiness about Martin Kelly was real and sharp. Unluckily there was no answer to it. He had the feeling, but he couldn't say why.

He looked up at the windows of Kelly's office as he departed. The morning sun hit them so that they showed nothing that was behind. It could be that nothing was there.

Coffin went to his meeting and met the great men. There were three of them: Reeve, Peters, and Savage. The Prime Minister was not there, but probably a tape was moving quietly in its hiding place, so that later he would hear everything that was said. Politics makes use of every modern technological aid. Ironically he called them that to himself. They were very polite, very smooth, and, he thought, showing unmistakable signs of tension.

They welcomed him and sat him down and gave him a drink in a friendly fashion. They were so friendly that in no time at all they were calling him John.

'Do you think you'll have this case wrapped up soon?' asked Savage, who seemed to be the spokesman. 'We all knew Barr and liked him. It's bad to think of this having happened.'

'I don't know yet who killed him,' admitted Coffin. 'But we're beginning to get an idea of the people involved.'

'Names?'

'I'd rather not just yet.'

'Give us what you can then.'

Coffin considered, adding what he knew. 'The killer was almost certainly a man. He sat for a time in a chair in the middle of the room and smoked a cigarette as if he was talking to them. He had previously sat or walked in the graveyard across the way and got earth on his shoes. At some stage a little of this earth got on to the girl Sheila's body, either from his hands or hers. It is possible the killer wore a paper mask.'

'Does that mean he was known to them?'

'He was known to them, I think, yes. But I don't think this was why he wore the mask. I don't know why he wore it.'

The whole killing sounds bizarre beyond words,' said Savage. 'And almost beyond reason.'

'There'll be a reason. Of sorts. Just as there will be a relationship between the killer and the dead when we can find it. The killer may have been more interested in Sheila Daly than Tom Barr.'

'Why do you say that?'

'The earth on her body,' admitted Coffin. 'At some point the murderer and she must have touched each other. Perhaps it was because of her he wore the mask. No, it won't do to overlook her part in everything.'

'I saw her once,' said Peters, speaking for the first time. 'She came up once with some letters for Tom. She certainly had something.'

The decanter of whisky remained on the table and he went over and poured more for himself. 'Have some,' he said. 'We need it. I don't know why, but the whole murder stinks. It smells of something corrupt, and devious, and terrible.'

'Kelly's back,' said Dove to Coffin as soon as he reentered the police building.

'I knew he would be.'

'We've got reports that he's visiting all houses in Great Barnabas Street and also those in the next few streets.'

'He's had a busy morning.'

'He only spends a few minutes. My man thinks he's really trying to identify a face.'

'Someone he's seen?'

'And doesn't know.'

'But wants to know?'

'That's it.'

'What he knows we want to know,' said Coffin. He hung up his coat. 'Well, get him in.'

'If we can,' said Dove. 'He knows how to disappear.'

'You'll get him this time,' said Coffin confidently. 'He's decided to surface. I think he wants to talk to us. He may not know it yet, but it's there in the back of his mind.'

'I hope you can convince him of that,' said Dove, disappearing.

Coffin drank some coffee from the thermos flask left on his desk and considered smoking a cigarette. But a round raw feeling in his diaphragm as the coffee filtered through convinced him that it would be a bad idea. 'Must have been hooch, that whisky,' he muttered to himself. 'And in the House of Commons too.'

The message about Martin Kelly went from Dove to the radio operator and from her to the patrol cars on the streets, and after them to the constables on the beat by means of their personal telephone equipment.

Coffin studied the reports on the Barr murder which had just come in, and the précis of other reports dealing with the other crimes in his manor which other officers were dealing with. Violent crime was up, up and up. Sooner or later he had to find out why. Or there'd be a Police Commission Enquiry waiting for him. Or he'd make the colour supplement of one of the Sunday newspapers.

He flipped over the papers, absorbing them quickly and dictating a note on tape for his typist where necessary. If he had to, he could work like an efficient machine himself. Now he was down to reading about the minor troubles of his bailiwick. A man had had a car stolen and it had turned up again painted yellow. A keg of yellow paint had been stolen from a shop down by the docks. That looked like cause and effect. Add to it the large boys' school also hard by, and you probably had the culprit too. Another man was complaining that his neighbour was running a cat farm in his back yard, and was using their fur to make fur hats. The other man denied it and said he just liked to have lots of cats around. The officer who had done a little delicate probing round (it was Policewoman Detective Joan Eames) reported that she thought there was something in the complaint but it was going to be difficult to prove. Post Office Engineers attempting to lay a new cable had discovered a tunnel leading from an empty house to the office block next door, which was owned by a bank. Someone had obviously been trying to mine their way in to the strong rooms. But the premises had ceased to be used for actual banking purposes ten years ago and the tunnel was an old one. 'There's no doubt about it,' murmured Coffin. 'In this district we have loonies like other areas have mice.'

Soon the telephone on his desk rang. It was Dove.

'We've located Kelly. He's sitting in the Mile End Café drinking coffee.'

'I hope he's feeling better on it than I am on mine,' said Coffin. 'Did they give him the message?'

'They did. And the answer is you can go and see him but he won't come and see you. The report was that he's in a surly mood. So it looks like your idea he wanted to talk was wrong.'

'I wasn't thinking of talking to Kelly personally,' said Coffin mildly. 'He and I never got along. What about one of the lads doing it? Or you?'

'Well, you know what he always thought of *me*. No, it's got to be you or nothing. If you think it's important.'

Coffin considered. 'It's important,' he decided. 'I don't want to speak to Kelly. Especially Kelly in a surly mood, but I'll go.'

'If your hurry,' said Dove, 'you'll just be in time for another cup of coffee.'

Coffin drove himself to meet Kelly. He drove slowly, thinking as he went. It was always well to have your thoughts in good order before meeting Kelly.

'Well, you came along,' said Kelly. He was in a sour mood all right.

'Yes, I came.'

'We met here once before. Remember? Seems ironical, doesn't it?'

'I don't see it that way.'

'No, you wouldn't. That time, I remember, I wanted something from you. Support, assistance, even the truth, call it what you like. This time, you want it from me.'

'I gave you the truth.'

'No, you didn't,' said Kelly, with a laugh. 'You said: Go on pretending with the Greginshaw mob until you find out what they're planning for St. Katherine's Docks. We'll look after you. You looked after me. The damn nearly killed me and I'm out of the Force because I can't pass my medical. And with the word going round I was bent and took three thousand pounds from Fats Greginshaw. That's how you looked after me.'

'Someone took three thousand pounds off him. I didn't start the rumour, it was you.'

'You believe it, though. Go on, it's written all over you. You put me on the job because you thought I was bent. It wasn't Greginshaw you were watching, but *me*.'

Coffin was silent.

'That's true, isn't it?'

'It's true.'

Kelly leaned back. 'I've been waiting a long time to

hear you say that aloud. And so you think you caught me?'

'I've never been quite sure,' said Coffin.

'Well, you'll never know now.' He sounded savagely satisfied. 'And now you've come to see me because you think I know something about the death of Tom Barr and Sheila Daly. Well, you're right again. I do.'

'I should hope you do, after watching him for three weeks at his wife's request. I should be disappointed if you didn't know *something*. You used to be a good detective.'

'I'm still a good detective. And still a sucker for the hard luck story, just like I was with you. You do this one for me, you said. You're the only one who can do it effectively, which in the circumstances I certainly was. This time it was Mrs. Camilla Barr. I think my husband's cheating on me, she said all the way from New York. You find out and I'll pay the bill. For what she was looking for,' he said bitterly, 'you couldn't pay the bill.'

'You were watching the house in Great Barnabas Street. I want to know what you saw. For a while you didn't want to tell me. Now I think you do. Something happened inside and you're quite willing to talk. You were there the night Thomas Barr and Sheila Daly were killed.'

'I was outside for about two hours on that night. They were alive when I left.'

'How do you know that?'

'I saw Sheila Daly at the window. She moved the curtain.'

'How well did you know Sheila Daly?'

'Not well. By sight only. I knew nothing about her before I started working on her.'

'And what do you know now?'

'Nothing much. She worked with Tom Barr. Also parttime at a hospital. That was voluntary.'

'How much did you watch *her*?'

'Hardly at all. I was concentrating on him.'

'And you're sure they were both alive when you left?'

'Yes.'

'Why were you there that night?'

'I knew it was the night the two of them were shut up together. I'd watched other Friday nights, but there was

never anything to see. People came and went. There were
less that particular night. A quiet night. Two men came.
I knew their faces, they were semi-regular visitors. The
third man walked across the road and went straight in
without knocking. I couldn't see him well. He had an
umbrella and a bag. It had been raining on and off all the
evening. He went in. Then after a short while he came out.
Then he went and sat in the graveyard. He sat there for
about fifteen minutes. Then he came back and went in
again. I left then.'

'And you think he was the murderer?'

'It's because I think he was I'm telling you now. I don't
want to suppress evidence.'

'Would you know him again if you saw him?'

Kelly shrugged. 'He was a man under an umbrella.'

'Camilla Barr is tall.'

'You mean was it really Camilla Barr dressed up as a
man?' He shrugged again. 'I admit the thought did cross
my mind. But I don't think so.'

Coffin paused to consider. At last they had a picture of
the killer: a man under an umbrella, walking into the
house, emerging to sit in the graveyard and then going
back in.

'So it's a man we're looking for,' he said aloud. 'Pity
you didn't get a better look. You didn't, did you?'

'No.'

'Quite sure you didn't?'

Kelly shook his head.

'All the same, you've been looking for him, haven't you?'

Kelly didn't answer.

'That's my guess,' said Coffin. 'And if you're looking,
then you think you have a chance of finding. You don't
waste your time. I'd call you a clever man. And you were a
good detective.'

'Thanks.' They studied each other with mutual distrust,
a distrust which had always been part of their relationship
and which had marked them both. From each it had taken
away a little. 'Got all you want out of me?'

'Not all, 'said Coffin rising to go now. 'Some to be going
on with. A few ideas. Such as that you tell some lies.'

Kelly smiled. He held up his hand. 'See you later then.'

'I know you, Kelly,' said Coffin. 'You're up to something. You haven't told me everything. Not by a long
chalk. What's on your mind?'

'There's nothing on my mind now. But later on I might
have an offer to make. Something for me in it and something for you . . .'

When Coffin had gone, Kelly paid for another cup of
coffee and took some sugar from the bowl on the counter.
It was the last spoonful.

'You need some more sugar,' he said to the counter
attendant, pushing it forward. The man filled it silently.

'I heard what you said to him.'

'Good. You'll make a fine witness,' said Kelly, swallow-
ing a mouthful of coffee.

'You're running a risk.'

'Negligible.'

'Not from him, I don't mean. Look, I can see the form.
I study human nature. I see what you're up to. You left
the Force. Not covered with glory.'

'We all know that.'

'Nothing proved.'

'Nothing to prove.'

'Well, so you say. Any road you've got a grievance. Now
you think you know a killer's name. You can trade that in
and they can offer you restitution. That's the word.'

'What's it mean?'

'It's a sort of revenge,' said the man doubtfully.

Kelly smiled. 'That's a good word, then.'

'And you told a lie. I reckon it could be dangerous.
Dangerous for you, I mean,' went on the man. 'The Police
could make it difficult for you,' he said seriously.

'Anything would be worth it,' said Kelly. 'Any risk—
to set things up the way I want.'

The warning notes were sounding, one after the other,
but none of the people concerned would listen to them.
Martin Kelly was too intent on his bargain. Camilla Barr
was still in a state of shock. Clem and his teacher Mark
were still absorbed in their quarrelling parent-teacher re-

lationship and were listening only to each other. John Plowman and his wife were getting the signals and might have interpreted them as well as anyone, but they were hardly in a position to be believed by the police. A ghost, they might have said, a paper man trying to get through.

Coffin couldn't hear them because he refused to believe in another world. He was a materialist and he wouldn't listen to ghosts.

There's none so deaf as those who won't hear.

He went for a walk past all the houses in Great Barnabas Street, looking at them and studying them.

14

Number two Great Barnabas Street was lived in by a family called Peeler. Numbers four to eight were sub-divided into one room apartments whose tenants came and went. Number ten belonged to a chiropodist who lived above his practice. Number twelve was where Thomas Barr and Sheila Daly had died. Numbers fourteen and sixteen were joined together as the hostel for theatrical children run by Mrs. Jolly where Mark Berkeley lived. All the houses had their own character. Number two was bright, numbers four to eight were seedy. Number ten had a brass plate and was strictly professional. The theatrical house was new painted and spotlessly clean: the colours were nursery colours, the whole effect rather like a children's merry-go-round. The house where Isaiah Steinberg had murdered his family and where Thomas Barr and Sheila Daly had died looked dull and respectable. Nothing marred its neatness and owner after owner (Tom Barr included) had been careful to keep the paint fresh. Once inside, the sensi-tive said it had a different feel, but Coffin had never been able to notice this himself. Nor could he find another police-man who had. Only Miss Jones said so. But strangely enough Miss Jones carried conviction. Perhaps this was be-cause she had taught him in nursery school. She lived round the corner from Great Barnabas Street and was delighted to have a call from Coffin.

'You don't remember,' said Miss Jones. 'But I entered your name on your first day at school.'

'I remember,' said Coffin.

'No, you don't.'

'I remembered someone,' said Coffin. What he remembered was a young girl with bright cheeks and red hair. Such a figure could have no connection with Miss Jones, thin, spare and grey, they couldn't be the same person.

'I always said I'd move away from here when I retired. I never liked the district.'

Like Camilla Barr, thought Coffin. 'How right you were,' he said aloud.

'I was a country girl, and it all seemed so noisy and dirty. And I didn't like the people. Not at first. So I always said I'd move. But I never did. Not even when the war came and it would have been easy. I went on residing. It's a world here, after all, you have to admit that.' She looked out of the window. 'Full of life. Every shade of goodness, all types of wickedness, you've got them all here.'

'You don't have to tell me.'

'*You* meet the bad ones. You don't see all the good. They don't come your way. There's a man down the Salter's Road Station. He's not old. I think he's a saint.'

'And John Plowman?'

'No, he's not a saint. He might be a seer though. They often have a hard time. You've got a touch of it yourself.'

'I certainly have a hard time.'

Miss Jones smiled. In her book the vigorous successful man had known nothing hard. What there had been of setbacks had only seemed to toughen him for the future. He had never been weakened.

'And what about Sheila Daly? You taught her too, didn't you? What was she?'

'I didn't teach Camilla Barr,' said Miss Jones. 'Sheila was a nice little girl. Easy to teach. Not like you. You were a wild one. She wasn't as clever as you, of course.'

'Thanks.'

'But she was more difficult to interpret.'

'Oh?'

'A natural poker face. Even as a little girl you could never be quite sure if she was pleased or unhappy. Basically, I don't think she was a happy little girl. But very willing and affectionate. Wanting to be loved.'

'I think she hadn't changed when she died,' said Coffin slowly.

'You don't change in that sort of thing. But it doesn't necessarily bring you happiness to be like that. And I don't think it did with her. She was an orphan, you know. An aunt brought her up. Then the aunt removed and went out to Australia and left Sheila behind. Sheila didn't like that. But she got on with her life, took a secretarial course in the city and went away.'

'Oh? She left the district?' Coffin pricked up his ears. 'You're the first person to tell me that. I thought she'd always been around.'

'She wasn't a girl that had many friends. And the one close friend she had was killed in a car accident.'

'Before Sheila went away?'

'Oh yes. Well before. And when she came back she was married. I've always wondered why she came back to live here?'

'Like you, like me, just couldn't keep away. Did you know her husband?'

'I saw them out shopping. He seemed a pleasant young man.' There was a restrained note in her voice which meant he hadn't made a good impression. Coffin knew the process. She was broadminded about dress and manners and quite willing to settle for your standards, rather than her own, but inside her she kept a sort of moral litmus paper against which to test you. If you came away the wrong colour you were silently judged. Coffin was always glad that he had taken the test at the age of five and apparently achieved the correct reaction. It was nice to have done it spontaneously and so young. And for life.

'And then he killed himself,' said Coffin, still hopefully probing.

Miss Jones shook her head. 'I don't know anything of that. He must have been sick.' A premature departure from this life was a weakness in her eyes, which, considering her great interest in other worlds and other minds might seem contradictory. But Miss Jones believed in a master plan for the universe and didn't think one should interfere with it.

'What did you have against him? Don't tell me there wasn't something?'

'Nothing I should really mind.'

'But something you do?'

'I suppose you'd say it was his appearance really. Something about his face. The quality of the skin. Almost as if it was used to having make-up on it.'

'Oh. Do you think *that* was what was wrong with Sheila and her husband?'

'Oh, I don't know,' said Miss Jones distastefully. 'I don't see that sort of thing as easily as your generation does. You're reading too much into what I said.'

'I thought I was reading what was there.'

'Sheila was a nice girl.'

'That's got nothing to do with it. Well, you've given me something to think about. Thanks.'

As he walked away he started thinking. It was all speculation, but sexual stress could be in the background of Sheila Daly's life. No one else had suggested it, but Miss Jones in the supermarket among the groceries had picked it up. And if so, he would have to focus more closely on Sheila Daly's life. Because a lot of the answers might lie there. He wanted to talk to someone, argue it out with them, but there was only the empty air, and the street cleaner brushing up the leaves. He stared down at the heap of leaves and rubbish hopefully, like a Roman augur assessing the entrails.

'Was the attacker out for Sheila Daly *first* and only took Tom Barr as an extra? Or was it Tom who was the object first, last and all the time?' He frowned. 'No it's more complicated than that, I swear.'

Coffin stared in the gutter at the heap of leaves, scraps of paper, cigarette ends and a banana skin.

'Lost something, guv?' The street cleaner came up.

Coffin shook his head silently, still staring on the ground.

'You won't find nothing there.' The cleaner pushed at the leaves with his broom.

'No,' Coffin straightened himself. 'Nothing.' He wasn't the sort of man to find the truth in the gutter.

As a seer he was a dead loss. Better visit John Plowman some time. He walked off.

* * *

The Plowmans were at high tea. Their back sitting room was a plain and pleasant place and this was where they ate at a round table. This room got the late afternoon sun and they liked to eat their main meal of the day enjoying it. They fasted all day, this being a hangover from one of their earlier faiths which they had got used to. Besides, it was an economy. But about five o'clock they got hungry.

'A little more fish, dear?'

'Thank you. I could manage it.' John passed his plate over.

'The maté's still hot,' said Mrs. Plowman, patting the pot. 'Another cup?' In another of their manifestations they had been vegetarians and herbalists, although nothing of this now remained except a taste for tisanes and green tea.

'Please.' He pushed his cup forward. They were both enjoying this lull in the day's activities. John Plowman had a surgery this evening. He always tried to be particularly relaxed before one of his evenings so that he could give his patients all his energies. That was what he said. He smiled at his wife and leaned back in his chair. There was honey in the comb on the table and sugar in its natural brown state. The bread was specially made from a strong wheaten flour. All these things cost just a little more than food more synthetic, but the Plowman household was enjoying a quiet prosperity these days.

'All going well, dear?' said Mrs. Plowman.

'Mm, yes,' he swallowed a mouthful of fish pie. 'This is good, dear.'

'I thought you looked a little worried.'

'Not consciously, dear. You know I try to erase all worrying thoughts before a session. I must give of my best.'

'Just a little bit more tension than usual,' persisted his wife. 'You didn't hear me the first time I asked if you wanted more fish. Hands a little tight, dear, neck muscles arched. Remember I'm competent to judge.'

'I know you are, my dear.' He swallowed a few more mouthfuls. 'Well, if I can put it this way, I'm having a patient.'

'Which patient?'

'Old Mark. Mark Berkeley.'

'Oh? His shoulder? Doesn't it improve? It seemed simple enough.'

'Not rheumatism in his arm. Not really. He's had a slight stroke there. He won't admit it. May not even know it.'

'Oh.' She was thoughtful and worried.

'He's got no strength in his arm. I had a word with Mrs. Jolly. Tactful, of course. Said I thought she ought to know. She had an idea of it, she said. Said it started about eighteen months ago with a slight shock.'

'Occlusion,' said his wife professionally. 'That's what we call it.'

'Yes, yes, that's what I meant.'

'And can you help him?'

'I can get some power back, not all.' He hesitated. 'There's a block in his mind. He's not co-operating.'

'What do you feel, dear?'

'Animosity,' said her husband simply.

She was at once alert. 'Against you, dear?'

Her husband sipped his tea. 'You know how it is in my relationship with my patients. If they don't love me they hate me. Often it's both at the same time.'

'It's really a compliment to your powers, John.'

'Yes, I know. But still. . . . He keeps making little jokes about how if I don't cure his shoulder he'll report me to the police for taking money under false pretences.'

'Oh, he wouldn't do that!' She was aghast. 'He's always been such a friend. Besides, you don't take money . . . Well, not really.'

'I could be attacked. The police don't like me. I'm a genuine believer, you see, and naturally that's the one thing they can't stand. But honestly, that's not what I'm worried about. It's him. I believe this murder has seriously disturbed him.'

'It's upset everybody,' said Mrs. Plowman.

'You too? Yes, I know,' he patted her hand. 'Still having trouble with a voice getting through?'

'I definitely feel there is a bad, bad mind in my ambience,' she said. 'And I can always tell. Sometimes I can absolutely feel it pressing on me.'

She put her hand on the teapot. Still hot. 'Another cup of tea, dear? To settle your mind before the evening.'

The hallway of the lodging house where Mark Berkeley lived with his friend and landlady, Mrs. Jolly, was always a place to meet people. If you were lonely, this was the place to be. There was always someone either coming in or going out, answering a telephone or looking for a letter. Mark knew this and although he would never admit the fact, he used it to assuage his loneliness. This evening he was lonely.

He went over to the letter rack, ostensibly to seek his post. He never had any. Joe Wolf, the young American student who was staying in the house, looked up from his own mail and smiled.

'Hi there.'

'Hello.'

'You don't look well. How are you feeling?'

'I'm feeling fine.'

'Well, if you say so. What about coming for a walk with me and dropping into the Blue Anchor? I like that pub.'

'Full of dock workers,' grunted Mark.

The other smiled. 'Well, what if it is? I've a good time there. Interesting talk. Interesting people. Come on.' And as Mark hesitated, 'You're low. You're brooding. I told you how it would be. Don't let things get on top of you.'

'I'm really going across to John Plowman to get some help with my arm.'

'Bad still, is it? You shouldn't rely on that old quack.'

'I could go later. I'll come round to the Blue Anchor with you.'

'You do that. I won't stay long. I have work to do.'

'What are you working at?'

'*On* more than *at*. Political history, German, French, English of the nineteenth century. Remember what Bismarck said at the Congress of Berlin: "The old Jew; that's the man to watch". He meant Disraeli. And remember what Disraeli said: "I bring you back peace with honour". Famous words. There's a lot of the political history of the nineteenth and twentieth century in those two phrases.'

'I like listening to you. I had a partner once with an American accent. Went down well on the halls.'

'Was that before you worked with your dummy?'

'No, I had the boy then. But we used to work it together.'

'You're fond of that old doll, aren't you? I hear you talking to it. Remember I've got the room next door.'

Mark looked discomfited. 'Just keeping in practice,' he said.

Mark did not go to see John Plowman that evening, and perhaps he got a little drunk at the Blue Anchor. At all events he came home later than the young American, who had left early to get back to his work.

His landlady heard him come in. Late again, she thought. I'll have to talk to him. I don't like the way things are going. I've got young people in this house. She turned over in bed. I'll get Clem to talk to him. Clem's closer to him these days than I am. Than I ever was. No one's got real close to Mark for a long time. Poor old Mark, him and that bloody dummy.

In the morning he slept late and his landlady, Mrs. Jolly, didn't disturb him. She looked in on him. The doll was lying propped up on a chair beside him, eyes closed. She looked at them both and then left them there.

Martin Kelly was walking back through the dark side passage to his office in the hour between ten and eleven when he first heard footsteps and then felt the hands on his throat. The grip was so gentle and tender that he felt confident of throwing it off, but although weak it was clinging in a way that baffled him. He struggled and writhed but the hands hung on in a soft elastic way that was throttling him.

'God, let go,' he grunted, trying to throw the attacker off but it clung like a sack. The figure behind him felt bulky without being heavy. He brought up his hands to try to pry the fingers loose. They were covered in what felt like soft padded gloves. The whole figure felt unreal, like a doll.

Strangely enough he knew at once who it was and why. 'I didn't know it would feel like this,' the thought moved hazily over his mind. 'Was this how it was for Tom and Sheila? No. It was different for them.'

Different because they were shot.

I knew you'd try to get me once I'd identified you, he thought. But I didn't know you'd try this. You're not human. With a tremendous effort he separated the fingers and swung round to meet his attacker. No, my God, you're not human. You doll you. He was dizzy and for a moment off balance. The padded hands of his attacker moved downwards. The figure took a step backwards.

Then he saw the gun in the padded hand. So it wasn't to be so unlike Tom and Sheila after all.

He tried to knock the gun down. 'Whoever taught you to go hunting?' he said.

The news about Kelly was given to Coffin with the first telephone call of the unwelcome day. Daylight and telephone call arrived almost together.

'What *is* the time?' he grunted, still half asleep.

'Past five. He was found three quarters of an hour ago. In the alley at the back of his office. Apparently he'd been dossing down there.' The speaker was an older detective, near retiring age. He had seen Kelly come and go in the Force.

'I know.'

'The ambulance man who took him in recognised him, knew him from the old days and the hospital got in touch with us. Thought he was still one of us, I suppose. Of course they would have reported anyway as it was a gunshot wound.'

'Who found him?'

'He found himself really. Crawled to a telephone box at the mouth of the alley and then dialled a call. He didn't speak, just dialled and left the receiver hanging. Then he crawled back to the alley. Goodness knows why. Didn't know what he was doing.'

'I expect there was a reason. There's always a reason. I've been in that sort of state or near it and whatever you do it's rational.'

'Anyway, he left a trail of blood and they found him. He's still alive, holding his own too. He's tough all right.'

'Said anything?'

'No, not yet. Not for some time, the doctors say.'

'And the bullet?'

'Well, it's still in him. He's in the operating theatre now.'

Later that day Coffin saw Martin Kelly. He was still unconscious, but the bullet had been extracted from his chest and he would probably live.

'He must know who shot him.' He looked at the doctor. 'When will I be able to question him?'

The doctor shrugged. 'I'll let you know about that.'

'I'd like it to be soon.'

'He may not remember anything much. That happens sometimes.'

Coffin looked down at the thin face. Even unconscious it looked determined.

'If anyone can he will,' he said. He turned to the doctor, 'What can you tell me about his wounds?'

'Shot in the chest from very close range indeed, I'd say.'

'So he certainly saw who shot him?'

'Saw, yes.' The doctor nodded to the nurse and took Coffin out.

He went back to his office where he continued with the routine of the day, moving easily into that world, apparently so real and yet so deeply cut into by fantasy that no police officer can emerge untouched. If one man's whole energies are directed at countering those of another man what he is doing really is to live that man's life. He is no more freed from the terrible compulsions of the murderer, the hopes of the big scale robbers, the desolations of the condemned than the men themselves. He knows them all. He thinks he is a professional man like a teacher or a doctor; he isn't. It's a black religion and he is the High Priest.

Within the hour the telephone at Coffin's left hand rang.

It was one of three on his desk and the one he liked the least. He had a theory that no good news came through that instrument. Whereas the one on his right, dexterous and good, brought news he wanted to hear. For a moment he ignored the left hand telephone. It went quiet. Then the right hand one rang. He picked up the receiver.

'Hello,' said Dove's aggravated voice. 'I think there's something wrong with the lines here. I had to switch. You didn't answer.'

'There's only one thing wrong with it.'

'What did you say?'

'What was it *you* wanted?'

'The same gun was used on Kelly as was used to kill Thomas Barr and Sheila Daly: 4.24 mm. A bullet from a German Lilliput. Surprised?'

'No. Not when I heard what the doctor said about Kelly's wounds.'

'What did he say?'

'That they were small.'

'If Kelly knows the killer and Kelly tells us, we're home, aren't we?'

Coffin was silent. 'If he talks.'

'Oh, he's going to live. I've had the hospital on the 'phone again. He's picking up fast.'

Again Coffin was silent.

He waited all day for the summons to visit Martin Kelly and when it came it was late afternoon.

Kelly was still in the same small room, but this time his eyes were open. They rested on Coffin remotely, as if looking well past him into a vista behind him. Impelled by them, Coffin looked over his shoulder. Nothing there, except the nurse and the doctor who stayed in the room with him.

'Hello,' he said softly.

Kelly's eyes shifted to his face.

'You look better.' He didn't; he looked whiter and much worse.

Coffin sat and said softly. 'Who shot you, Kelly? You know who it was. Let *me* know.'

Their eyes met. Deep, deep down behind the dark contracted pupil and blue iris he fancied he could read something in Kelly's eyes. He drew back.

'Don't tell me you're clinging to this idea of a bargain. Be reasonable. You nearly got killed. Who was it?'

Kelly said nothing.

'It was a man, wasn't it?'

'I think so. Not sure.'

'I'm not allowed to talk to you much. Soon I'll have to go. Give me something. Anything.'

Something remotely like a smile flitted across the other man's face.

'Well, I can't,' he said.

'You mean you can't remember?' There was a nod. 'All right, let's take it bit by bit. You had bruises on your throat, so someone had their hands on you. You must have wrenched them off and then swung round. What were the hands like?'

Kelly thought. 'Padded,' he said.

'Padded?' Coffin was taken aback. 'Thick gloves, you mean?'

'Padded.'

'I see. I'll have to think that out. But thanks. Now, after this, you must have seen the face? Who was it?'

This time he knew without doubt what he was seeing on Kelly's face. The lines of rigid determination appeared there, deepened by fatigue and pain. Behind it, a very faint line of amusement.

'Didn't see,' he said.

From the door the doctor said: 'I think that's enough for now.'

'Goodbye,' said Coffin, leaning down to say it.

'Come back later, alone,' said Kelly in a barely audible voice. 'Come back with an offer and we might do a deal.'

'You look troubled,' said his wife that night.

'I'm troubled.'

'Oh well, I won't ask questions.'

'And I couldn't answer them if you did.'

'You think I'd talk outside?' She was hurt.

'No, I meant that I couldn't answer questions because

I don't know the answers. I just have the feeling that there's one great muddy pool and someone's moving the mud around with a stick.'

'I heard about Martin Kelly,' said his wife. 'I thought I might go and see him. Would you mind?'

'Leave it.'

'So you would mind.'

'Not the way you think. Leave it for now. If I want you to go, I might ask you, and give you a message to take.'

'He's madly sexy, old Martin. I've always thought that was why you hated him so much.'

'Is that what people are saying? Her boy friend?'

'Yes. You never hear anything. A real femme fatale, that's Camilla.'

'Thanks.'

'On second thoughts, I won't hurry down. I might meet Camilla Barr there and she and I have never been friends. She isn't lucky, is she? Her husband and now her boy friend.'

Automatically earlier that day the police had checked on the movements of all who could be thought to have contact with both Thomas Barr and Sheila Daly and Martin Kelly.

This was how Camilla Barr heard the news. She came to the door of her apartment, nursing a small dog. She was wearing a red velvet trouser suit and managed to look chic and cool. The shadow under her cheekbones became more pronounced as she listened.

'I'm sorry he's hurt. No, we didn't have any contact yesterday. I had no idea of his movements.'

She watched the policeman go away and went back to her cousin, who was sitting smoking.

'Why did you say that, Cam? You did see him yesterday.'

'Not important.' Camilla put the dog down.

'The police'll think so if they find out.'

'What they don't find out won't hurt them.'

'Cam, sometimes I think you're crazy,' said Jen.

'Yes, I am,' said Camilla, lighting a cigarette. 'Hard, cold and crazy. It's the modern disease.'

The little dog came up and sat on her bed. He licked her hand.

Clem Grove heard about Martin Kelly in the Museum where he was placidly working.

'I've been here all day,' he said. 'No, I don't suppose anyone's seen me here.' He looked at his crowded desk. 'I've had an awful lot to get through. I've just stuck. Yes, last night, too. I was working late. The light would be on. I dare say that would be seen.'

'I saw it myself, sir,' said the detective who was talking to him (it was hard to use the word questioning of Clem, who was so gently informative). 'I was walking home late.'

'Well, there you are then.' Clem smiled and spread his hands.

'You knew Mr. Kelly?'

'He came down this street calling at all the houses,' said Clem. 'So we saw each other even if we didn't know each other. He came in here and pretended to be looking at things in the Museum. Perhaps he even was looking at them. The strangest people show an interest. And it's free, of course,' he added with mild irony.

Mrs. Jolly saw the police and said her lodger had come in late last night and was still in bed. He was asleep and she wasn't going to wake him up. She didn't think he was up to much. Baffled, the detective went away, promising to return.

'Not up to much,' murmured Mrs. Jolly, going to her lodger's door and listening. 'You're up to too much.'

She could hear the murmur of his voice as he talked inside the room. She couldn't quite hear what he said. Or what it said. He, she or it, whatever it was.

Mark paused in his speaking. He could hear her very well at the door. He knew her little trick of pausing to listen before coming in. He gave his model a pat and put it back in the cupboard.

'Well, you didn't do too well,' he said. 'I hope you know that. A failure, really. Better next time, eh?'

Mrs. Jolly pushed open the door, just at the moment he

had known she would. His sense of timing had always been impeccable.

'Silly old thing,' she said. 'Why don't you give up all this practice? What are you hoping for?'

Mark answered hesitantly, as if he wanted her to hear the truth. 'We still have a relationship. But hopes? No. Practice? Well, no, Doris, not quite what you think.'

Mrs. Jolly shut the door and went on down the stairs, frowning.

Her young American visitor was in the hall.

'Anything wrong, Mrs. Jolly?' he asked.

'I'm worried about Mr. Berkeley, I think I shall have to let him go. He's upsetting the tone of the house.'

'Oh no,' said the young man with genuine sympathy.

'He's living in a dream world. A dream of his comeback.' She shook her head. 'You wouldn't know. Americans are so practical.'

He laughed. 'Look at our newspapers. Study the advertisements, see what they show you about the great American dream.'

'Of course, we're all upset now. I can't just blame Mark.' She began to fiddle with the flowers in a vase on the table.

'Well, death coming like that is bound to distress anyone.'

'Yes. It seems to grow and grow in my mind.'

'I know.' He nodded.

'What happened there? What *really* happened? That's what I keep thinking all the time.'

'Don't think about it.'

'I try not to.' She picked up the flowers. 'Those are dead.'

'I've got my passage booked home.'

'Oh, good. I know it's been worrying you.'

'Well, one likes to get things settled.'

The American Senator's dream was troubled. Just lately he had but the one dream, an unusual symptom in itself. And then it was such a disturbing dream. More it was a brilliant, provocative, stimulating dream.

However, it wasn't the dream to wake up with and to go

to work on on a bleak morning. Over breakfast, which they took together, his wife commented on his mood.

'I don't think you're well.'

'I'm quite well, dear.'

'You were tossing and thrashing around in your sleep. And talking too. That's not right.'

'What did I say?'

'Nothing I could catch.'

Well, that's something anyway, he thought, returning to his breakfast. In his newspaper he read the account of the investigation into the death of Tom Barr, M.P., in London. It sounded a dirty business.

'Didn't we meet this man's wife sometime?' he said.

'What man?'

'The British M.P., Barr, who's been murdered.'

'Oh yes, once at a party.' She dismissed the subject and went back to what really interested her. 'I don't think it's normal to have nightmares.'

That was no nightmare, he thought, that was a beautiful roaring, rumbustious dream. I was the all-American male. Was there a mare in the dream? The image darted rapidly and savagely into his mind. There had been animals present. Suddenly, it all seemed bestial and he was ashamed.

'*Now* what's the matter?' said his wife.

'Why nothing.' It was only a dream.

'You changed colour.' She was puzzled and doubtful. He saw she would have to be given something to placate her.

'I'm sorry, dear. Perhaps I do feel a little not myself.' That put it in a nutshell and was also true. 'But breakfast is helping.'

'It's the second night running,' she said accusingly. 'And you don't make love to me any more. Why don't you? Have you got someone else?'

He put down his cup and sat quite still. He was deeply shaken. 'I didn't know. I didn't mean . . . I hadn't noticed,' he started.

'You didn't notice?' Her voice rose. 'You certainly are sick.'

It's a dream he wanted to say. But how could you say

to your wife that in your dream you were making love to a great beautiful woman. Only not her. No resemblance at all.

Dreams fade so quickly; the details of his dream were fading already, but he had suddenly the distinct impression that at some point in their animated intercourse the beautiful lady had become a beautiful man.

That really was sick.

He was beginning to realise that there could be a seepage from the dream to this world of the day. His body, which changed colour and gulped the coffee and shouted in its sleep, was realising it before his mind, that practical ambitious, bemused organ.

Supposing the sort of thing that had happened to Tom Barr, happened to him?

On that night they died Sheila and Tom Barr finished their first stint of work, talked about the fact that Camilla Barr, Tom's wife was having him watched, and then went back to work.

Three business telephone calls interrupted them.

The room was hot, Tom not well (he had already taken some aspirin) and Sheila on edge. She went to get a drink of water. Thirst with her was often a sign of tension.

Shortly after this came one telephone call which Sheila did not like because the caller hung up without speaking.

But this happened occasionally. They both knew it, and they settled back to work, not relaxing but willing to keep on with the job.

'I thought you said there was no one outside,' said Thomas.

Sheila shook her head with a slight smile. 'There wasn't.' It was a matter of habit with her to check the outer waiting room for callers.

'There's someone there now.' He went to see who it was.'

'Hello,' he said to the visitor. 'I didn't expect you.'

'I'm sorry if I've disturbed you.'

'Oh no, not disturbed,' said Tom. 'This is my night for seeing people.'

'That's what I thought. I just walked in.'

'Of course.' Tom was always over hearty when he was ill at ease. 'This isn't a closed door, you know. I like to see people. It's the job.'

'On political matters?'

'On anything I can help them with.'

There was a pause, then: 'You can help me.'

'Well, come along into the other room,' said Tom, still heartily, 'and we can talk. In case someone else comes in here.'

'Oh no one will come. I've put the latch down on the door.'

Tom was startled. 'You have. Well, I don't know. . . .'

'We usually lock up about now,' said Sheila, coming to the door.

'Yes, so we do,' said Tom, still polite, if increasingly puzzled by his caller. But he didn't want to hurt anyone's feelings. There was usually a rational explanation for behaviour. Or so he hoped.

The three of them moved back into the inner room and the door was shut.

He went and sat down at his desk. 'Now, what can we do?' He looked. 'Would you like to put your bag down?'

'No, I'll keep it on my lap.'

He really is awkward for someone in what you could call public life, thought Tom, the public eye anyway. He was always having to meet people, talk to them and at them. Strange to be so gauche. If that was what it really was.

'I haven't been quite open with you. I didn't really come round here because I wanted help for myself. No. I came to help you.'

'Me?'

'Well, both of you.' He looked round towards Sheila. Tom did not answer.

'I'll go outside,' said Sheila. 'I don't want to listen.'

'Everyone's saying you two have been mucking about.'

Tom thought: 'God, he's quite coarse underneath. That sophistication on top covers something cheap.'

The other man saw that he'd given something away and

said quickly, 'I'm using the words they use round here, of course.'

'Thanks,' said Tom. 'But I don't believe you.'

'Oh, I assure you it's true.'

'I don't have to listen,' said Sheila, getting up. 'You make me ill. I think you're sick yourself. There's a name for that sort of thing.'

'I didn't more than half believe it when I came here. Now I do.'

'That's nonsense,' said Tom. He too stood up. 'I don't know what you're thinking of.'

'Look at her,' he nodded towards Sheila's flushed face. 'That'll tell you what I'm thinking of. Look at her. She gives it away.'

'I ought to hit you,' said Tom.

'That'd look fine,' he said. 'M.P. brawling over woman. You've got to watch your temper.'

'Please go. I'll give you the benefit of the doubt, maybe you mean well, but just go. Can't you see you're upsetting Sheila?'

'I'm going now.' He got up. 'I'll leave the door unlocked.'

They waited to hear the door click before moving.

An insect was buzzing round the centre light. Sheila moved towards the window as if to close it against the entrance of any more. There was a line of sweat on her face.

She sat down and put a hand to her head.

'My dear,' said Thomas, turning back to her.

'I'm sorry.' She put her head right down. 'I feel sick.'

'I'm sorry, terribly sorry to have involved you in all this.'

'No. Not you, it's me,' she mumbled. 'Don't you see that. No.' She sat up.

'Are you feeling faint?' He moved to her side.

'No, it's my hands. They've got dirt on them.'

The front door banged again. They both heard it.

'Don't say anything,' said Thomas. 'Don't, don't say anything.'

15

On the next day, the surprising thing happened and they had some information about the gun. The German Lilliput is not a usual gun and people who have had one in their possession are not likely to forget it. But not all the people the police were questioning were free with their memories. Sometimes it was safer to forget. Tucked away behind the Blue Anchor public house was a small junk and curio shop. It was an object of occasional scrutiny by the police. The proprietor was usually willing to give what help he could to an enquiry. He carried on a small and furtive trade as a police informer.

Since he was a nervous and cautious man it often took him some time to get in touch with the police about any information he might have. This time he waited until a detective called.

'Oh, um, I've been thinking.' He moved a brass vase from one shelf to another, then back again.

'Come on, Jimmy, then, let's have it.'

'Oh yes.' He fidgeted with some papers on an old-fashioned wooden counter in front of him. He very rarely sold anything, but the apparatus for selling, counter and cash register and willing hands, was all there. 'How much will it be?'

'It depends on what the news is, Jimmy. Now you know that.' This sort of jocular bargaining was automatic between them. 'Times are hard.'

Jimmy looked down at his hands; they always trembled a little, but when he stared hard at them the trembling stopped. He stopped concentrating on his hands and the trembling started again. 'You know that gun you've been enquiring about?'

'The 4.24 German Lilliput? Yes.'

'You never came to me about it.'

'Give me time. I was coming. I'm here now. Anyway, you don't usually wait behind the door.'

'Murder weapon, was it?'

The detective was silent.

'That's what they say,' said Jimmy. 'It's what I thought.'

'Supposing it was, then?'

'It's still on the loose, isn't it? You haven't got it?'

'No.'

'Makes me nervous, that.'

'No reason to believe it'll come pointing at you, Jimmy, is there?'

'Ah, but it might. I believe I saw it.'

'Go on. I'm interested.' He took out a packet of cigarettes. 'Have a smoke?'

'Thanks, I will. I didn't know what it was, mind. Not then. Thought it was a kid's toy.'

'Some kid.' Jimmy's left hand was keeping up a steady drumming on the wooden counter. 'Control those hands, Jimmy, I can't hear myself think.'

'I saw a gun could be it. Sammy Rough had it. Brought it out of his pocket and put it on the table in front of him.'

'Sam Rough? Sammy Rough, eh?'

'You're not suggesting *he* done it, are you?' said Jimmy, his hands calming as his interest mounted. 'He's inside. Went in six weeks ago for knocking off a fur dealer in a shop in the Lambeth Road. Robbery with violence that was. Only he never uses a gun. I told you that was a toy.'

'The one place we never thought of looking for the gun was in prison,' said Coffin when he was told. 'Well, we can try. It could be the gun.'

'I've never known Jimmy wrong,' said the detective who had brought the news in. 'Often he's slow about talking, but anything you get is genuine. I reckon he's got telepathy.'

'I must introduce him to an old friend of mine called Jones,' said Coffin.

In prison, Sammy Rough, a small sturdy man with a crooked nose, was interviewed. He was willing to talk about the gun. It seemed to rankle.

'Yes, I had a Lilliput. Brought it back from Germany when I'd been over.'

'What were you over there for, Sam?'

'Winter sports,' said Sam, with a straight face. 'Brought it back. Thought it might amuse my girl friend. She didn't like it.'

'Was that when she broke your nose? I think I heard about that.'

'Hit me over the nose with it. Said she wanted a mink stole.'

'And where's the gun now?'

'Didn't sell it,' said Sam. 'That would be a criminal offence. I know better than that.'

'So?'

'Didn't even give it away. No. It was stolen.'

'Go on,' said the detective scoffingly.

'Well, he paid £5 for it. Worth twenty. That *was* stealing.'

'Who was it?'

'Dunno his name. Met him in the Blue Anchor. He knew I had a gun.'

The detective looked at him, assessing the situation. 'He'd heard you had a gun going?'

'He might have done, yes.'

'You had met him before?'

'I can't say.'

'But you'd know him if you saw him again?'

'I couldn't promise. You know what my eyesight's like.'

'Comes and goes as it suits you.'

'No, I'm genuinely short sighted. Ask the doctor.'

'You always let me lean on you a little,' said the detective; he looked menacing.

'O.K., O.K., no threats.'

'I wouldn't touch you.'

'Who said? All I can remember is that he was an older man, looked as though he took care of himself though. Hair wasn't grey. Dyed, I should think. It didn't *look*

dyed, so it was a professional job. But I was apprenticed
to a hairdresser when I was a kid.'

'You know more than that.'

Sam shrugged. 'That's all for now.'

The detective got up. 'Why didn't you stay in hairdressing?'

'Know what they paid me? Thirty bob a week. That's
why I didn't stay in hairdressing.'

'And what do you get in here?' said the detective.

'Know what I've got outside?' said Sam slyly.

'I know what you *think* you've got stashed away. But
you and I know what can happen to these little squirrel
hoards. The big birds eat them.'

'O.K.' said Sam. 'I had heard rumours. Tell you what:
you check up for me and I'll give you my little bit extra.'

'Well, your mink stole has gone to the Channel Islands.
Several thousand pounds in hard currency went with it.'

Sam swore. 'Any more? Well, get what you can. Remember, you're working for me. This is for you: the old
boy who bought the gun was called Mark. I never got any
more, but remember this: Mark.'

Mark was playing with his dummy. If you could call it
that. It was hardly play and yet it was certainly play-
acting.

To himself he called it rehearsing.

'Now, my dear,' he said, propping the dummy up in the
chair in front of him. 'Let you and I talk to each other.
Come on now, speak up. You're slow today.'

The puppet remained silent.

'No sulking,' said Mark, in a sprightly manner, as if
he really enjoyed reprimanding his doll. 'I had to give you
a reproof. Well and good. That wasn't a successful attempt.
You didn't do well. You have to try again. There's no half-
way house about killing someone. If you cannot do it
properly you might as well not try at all.'

There was still silence. Perhaps a little croaking noise
from the direction of the doll. It was a preparation for
speech. You might say it was warming up.

'Now say after me: Hello, Camilla.'

'Hello, Camilla,' piped the dummy, not very convincingly.

'We're out of practice,' said Mark jovially. 'That wasn't good at all.'

'I'm glad to see you, Camilla,' said the creature.

'That's better. You must sound glad. Because you are glad. For reasons she doesn't know about yet.' He laughed. 'Say, come over here, Camilla, so I can talk to you.'

'Come over here, Camilla, so I can talk to you.' It was hardly beguiling: Camilla wouldn't have budged. 'Cammy, Cammy.'

'No, you don't call her Cammy,' said Mark. 'That's what the cousin calls her. You're not the cousin.'

'I bet I could be,' said the dummy with a snigger.

'No, you couldn't be,' said Mark sharply. 'Even you can't change your sex.' Then he too laughed. 'Know what? We ought to be on the stage.' Then they both laughed. That is, they only had one voice between them, but somehow they managed it.

'Please, dearest Camilla, there is something I have to tell you,' said the dummy.

'Very nice,' said Mark. 'You are on those terms, I suppose? You can call her dearest Camilla?'

The dummy didn't answer, didn't know the answer probably.

'Yes, I guess you are,' said Mark thoughtfully. 'In your sort of class, with your sort of person, the word "darling" means nothing. We're not making much progress. What I mean is, if I may think aloud . . .'

'Don't you always?' said the dummy.

'Don't I always,' agreed Mark. 'But what I mean is I don't think I'm giving you the right cues.'

'Oh, pardon me,' said the dummy.

'Shut up,' said Mark. 'I'm thinking . . .'

There was dead silence. Silence was wrong on a stage and it clearly worried them both.

The dummy started to hum a song. Then broke off.

'This isn't a *performance*,' said Mark. 'I'm rehearsing.' The doll slid forward in the chair and he moved it back with his foot, not gently. Not gently at all.

'It's not you I want to hurt,' said Mark.

The dummy sniggered. It seemed involuntary.

'Well, maybe I do a bit,' said Mark. 'I want to hurt someone. So it might as well be you.'

He sat down beside the dummy, there was just room for them both in the armchair; it squeezed the dummy a bit, but who cared?

'The thing is,' said Mark, 'it's so awfully difficult (and getting more difficult each time) to get the word Kill across. I thought it would get easier. But no, harder. There is a block. Whether it is in me or you I am unable to decide.'

There was another pause in which it was audibly his voice which hummed the tune and not the dummy's.

'Kill,' said Mark thoughtfully. 'You must kill Camilla. I might just as well come right out and say it. Kill Camilla. I wish I could say use the gun, but no: prudence must prevail. I have to think of myself. You must do it by hand. Got that. *Do it by hand.*'

Then he added thoughtfully: 'I wonder if those hands *could* damage anyone's throat, let alone throttle them.' Absently, he picked up one of the dummy's limp hands.

'It's supposed to be you won't do anything you don't really want to do. That's the theory. But I feel this block. The channel of communication between me and thou does not run clear.'

'You and me and thou and whoever you are,' he said dreamily.

Kill Camilla, kill Camilla. Music had power, perhaps music added to words could do the trick. Kill Camilla. Kill Camilla. Barr, Barr, black sheep.

His landlady banged on the door. 'Are you mad in there, singing like that?'

'Sorry,' said Mark, hoping she could not hear the words. Then he went to the door and threw it open. 'I'm rehearsing. Rehearsing,' he shouted. 'And when Clem comes, show him up.'

16

The detective who had interviewed Sam Rough in prison was a new man to the area so that the name Mark did not sound an alarm in his mind. He had a name to put in his report and a lead to follow and with this he was satisfied. On the way back from the prison, which was out of London, he saw a child fall off a bike and under a lorry. This took the edge off his concentration. And when he arrived back at the duty station, reports were just coming in of a big robbery down by the docks, which was complicated by suspected arson. He found some extra work being thrown at him. However, he remembered to put in his report on Sam Rough first.

His seniors were also dealing with the dock robbery and also receiving the news that six prize greyhounds had been stolen from a local kennels. It was evening before Coffin read the report himself. At once he telephoned Dove.

'You've read what the boy got from Sam Rough?'

'Of course.'

'What did you do?'

'I sent a man round to look at the house. See what Mark Berkeley was doing. He's still there. The landlady, Mrs. Jolly, says he's been rehearsing and giving a speech training session. That's just the beginning. Tomorrow we go on from there.'

'There's still tonight. I hate waiting.'

'I'll keep a check on the house. Just to see what goes on. It'll be a quiet night, you'll see.'

'The quiet nights are the worst.'

'No, they're not,' said Dove, who had a very straightforward mind. 'Not in my book.'

When they had finished, Coffin went downstairs to the room which was still the principal headquarters for the team investigating the murder of Thomas Barr and Sheila Daly. The staircase was quiet and dim, alternate lights being turned off to mark the end of the working day. Only hardly anyone stopped working.

There was one man sorting papers at a long table in the Barr-Daly room. This room would never be left entirely unstaffed until the case was closed.

The man, a young detective, looked up but did not say anything, waiting for Coffin to speak first. He had a drawn look as if he was tired, but his dark hair was neat and his face newly shaved. Coffin at once felt old and seedy. It truly was a sign of age when fatigue made you look, not strained, but dirty.

'Don't let me disturb you. I just want to look around.' He made his way over to a set of drawers, opened the top one and drew out a plain brown paper bag. Out of the bag he took the mask found in the rubbish bin in the old graveyard.

He had examined it carefully several times already, and the forensic scientist had had a go. There was no proof that it had been used by the killer, just a very strong suggestion it might have been. Face outwards it was a simple childish affair. On the inside was a smear, broken into two parts, one long and thin, the other short, a mere blob. At first it had looked like blood, but it wasn't.

The laboratory workers had identified it as an emulsified make-up base in a shade they named loosely as 'dark natural', which meant that they thought the person who had worn it hadn't looked strikingly made-up. 'Either sex' they had added, neutrally.

As far as any conclusion had been drawn from it the police had decided that at some point the inside of the mask had been in touch with Sheila Daly's face. Possible she had worn it.

'I don't believe she did,' decided Coffin. 'She was a blonde. Her make-up colour would be too creamy. The murderer wore it. Mark Berkeley could have worn it. He had been an actor. I'm not saying he wears make-up. I've never noticed any on his face. But he could have some about him. Could have been in contact with make-up. Something left over from his past life.'

When they looked for the gun in Mark Berkeley's room, then they might look for some bottles of make-up too, and see if they could make a match.

'Wonder how it all fits in?' he said, and he must have said it aloud because the other man at the table down the room looked up quickly. 'Nothing,' said Coffin, turning away.

He put the mask back in its paper bag and returned them both to the drawer. Perhaps he had been hoping that physical contact with the object would produce some ideas. But nothing came.

He went slowly out of the room, collected his things and started to walk home through the quiet side streets. And all the time a thought was quietly making its way up from his finger tips to his brain.

Rain had just fallen and even this city back street had a sweet fresh smell. The lamplight falling on the few trees made their leaves look a dramatic green.

To Coffin at the moment, tired and perceptive, it looked like a stage set. The actors might, at any moment, come strutting out on to the scene. He went to the theatre regularly because he was married to an actress. It was natural for him to think in terms of the theatre.

In addition, he and Tom Barr had been among the chief supporters of the Repertory Company established in the old music hall. They had sat on the committee together, Coffin not saying much.

The thought was coming very close to the surface of his mind now. He could even feel the outriders of it. Orange peel and dates. Laughter in a crowded place. The memory of a light focused on one round cheerful face. A spotlight.

'Good Lord,' thought Coffin. 'So *that* was Charlie Grinling.'

Immediately he got home he ignored the cat crying from the kitchen and his wife calling from the stairs and went straight to the telephone.

'I know who Charlie Grinling is,' he announced at once to Dove.

Dove groaned. 'Don't tell me he's living next door.'

'He's a local boy all right. But he was internationally known. Well, that was how he was always billed.'

'Billed?'

'Yes, he was Mark Berkeley's dummy. Charlie Grinling and Mark they were called. And he did have a great big grin on his face. I remember seeing them at the old music hall. So we wipe out thoughts of all other Charlies, like the Charlie Colver, and concentrate on *this* one.'

'You aren't suggesting *he* killed Barr and Daly?'

'I'm suggesting that his name came into Sheila Daly's mind as she was dying.'

'Yes, I agree we could dig around and find out more about Daly,' said Dove. 'She seems to have been the girl nobody knows. Still, it begins to look like Mark Berkeley, doesn't it? Do you think he dressed up like his dummy? Or took it with him?'

'Or sent it instead,' said Coffin.

'What a horrible thought.'

'I have horrible thoughts,' said Coffin, and put the receiver down. He had gripped the receiver hard, so it was hot where his hand held it. The same hand had held the mask which the murderer had held. He looked down at it. No trace of the smear of make-up was on his hand, nothing was there to show. But some faint smell must somehow have got attached to him. Enough to remind him of the smell of grease-paint, the laughter of the music hall, and to summon up the ghost of Charlie Grinling. You *could* receive knowledge through your fingertips. Telemetry, people like Miss Jones called it.

The little boys in Mrs. Jolly's boarding house were restless that night. At all times they were an over-strung, nervous group. About half of them were working in the chorus of a big musical just preparing to go on tour and the rest were attending drama school and auditioning, putting their hearts into each about equally.

The murders had affected them profoundly, more even

than with ordinary children; these were alert, sophisticated superstitious creatures.

That evening they gathered in the sitting room, watching the late programme on the television. They were all night birds, not going to bed until exhausted. This night they sat on and on. Mrs. Jolly looked in on them but only made a mild suggestion that they go to bed.

'We've got to unwind, Aunty,' one of them said. 'Can't sleep till I'm unwound.'

'It always takes me hours to let down,' said another. 'Guess I'm just naturally tense.'

'Ah, you can't help it,' said another. 'If you're a performer you're a performer. You're spinning it all out of yourself, what can you expect?'

'I can't go to bed yet,' said the first speaker. 'Not to sleep, that is. I should only lie there all tense. Feel my hands, feel how tense they are. I gotta learn relaxation. I'm working on it, going to classes. It's hard for me.'

They were a hard-boiled, travelled little lot, they knew everything. But it didn't stop their imaginations working overtime. A story was going around, whispered from boy to boy. A ghost was walking.

'Anyone working in the theatre's bound to believe in ghosts,' said the first boy. 'Living on nerves like we do. Projecting all the time, we're naturals for a haunting. I mean our minds are open, aren't they? We drain ourselves.'

'Speak for yourself,' said a friend. 'I've got stamina. I'm not drained.'

'Well, I've got stamina too,' said the other boy irritably. 'You've got to have in this life. But we're sensitive. You admit that? We're sensitive. So we feel. This story about the ghost is bound to get us. I don't say I believe. I've got an open mind.'

'Oh, I believe,' said another, with a shiver. 'I think I saw it. Him, I mean. Last night.'

'Oh, go on, what was it like?'

'A dark figure. Sitting hunched up. Not like a real person at all. More like a shadow.'

'Where was it?'

'In the old churchyard, of course, where else?'

'Yeah, that's true,' said a voice. 'Where else?'

'Could be,' said someone.

'It was. I tell you. And I wasn't alone. Mr. Wolf was with me. He saw it first.'

Mr. Wolf was working quietly at a table at the other end of the room, as usual, but they interrupted him.

'Mr. Wolf, Mr. Wolf, did you see it?'

Mr. Wolf obligingly put down his book. 'Yes, I saw something. But a ghost? Who can say. But it certainly was a strange time to be sitting in the old churchyard. I mean if you think about it, last night was a wet night and dark too.'

'And the way it disappeared, Mr. Wolf, remember that?' said the boy who had told the story. 'I mean it looked like a shadow all the time except that it was sort of solid, and then it just faded, didn't it? One minute it was here and then just the lamplight on the seat.'

'Perhaps it was the street light and a shadow all the time.'

'You didn't think that, Mr. Wolf, did you? I know you didn't. I could *feel* what you were thinking. A ghost, that was in your mind.'

Mr. Wolf appeared to hesitate. 'Well, momentarily, Brian, perhaps,' he admitted. 'Excuse me,' he said. He got up and went out.

'He left us so we could talk,' said the boy called Brian. 'Very tactful, he is, Mr. Wolf.'

'He knows what we'll talk about.'

'If a ghost killed those people, which I don't say I believe, mind, then what's to stop him coming in here and doing us?'

'But ghosts aren't real,' said one. 'It's all in the mind. They can't actually touch you.'

'If I saw a ghost I'd die,' said one thin young lad. 'Just die. He wouldn't have to touch me.'

'Bury me deep,' said someone. 'I don't want to get up and walk around.'

'It doesn't have to be a ghost walking round killing

people,' said the thoughtful boy. 'I mean a ghost may not have to work that way. It could be working through us.'

'What's that?'

'In our profession we know all about influencing people's minds, don't we? A spirit seeking revenge could operate through us. A mind can influence another.'

'What a horrid idea.' Someone threw a cushion at him. A fight started. But it was really to create a distraction. Inside they were deeply shocked.

This conversation was later reported to the police by Mrs. Jolly, who got it from one of the boys. It is all in the police records. Nothing was ever made of it. Yet it was there. Much later Coffin read it. And wondered.

Camilla was restless like the boys. The little dog with her was uneasy as well. Jen was away for the night, and the two remaining creatures roamed restlessly round the apartment.

The dog yawned. 'I *could* sleep,' the yawn seemed to say, 'if only you'd settle down and let me.'

Then the dog moved his head sharply and looked up.

'What's that, Silver?'

Silver barked under his breath, listened again and then followed this up with a low growl. This was his speciality. It was a natural gift; he hadn't invented it or perfected it, although obviously it was a comfort and a pleasure to him. Jen called it his warning growl.

'What is it, Silver? You're alarming me.'

Silver got up and walked to the door. He was listening. Camilla looked at Silver doubtfully, then went to the sitting room door and listened too. 'I don't hear anything,' she said.

The hall outside was dark.

'Thought I left the light on,' said Camilla. 'I suppose Jen turned it off.' She flipped it on and went back to the sitting room.

She was wearing a tunic of stiff silk with matching trousers. 'Some mourning,' she thought, catching sight of herself in the mirror. She sank back into her chair, picked up her book and tried to read. It was a book of Tom's, a war history, the last days of Berlin as the Russians came in. Tom had annotated it with small, neat pencil observations. Probably it was a review copy.

The sight of his writing was painful to her. For the first time she remembered their early years together, before they were married. She could remember the first letter he had ever written her, a mere note, scrawled on a piece of rough paper. As soon as she had read it she had known he could be a friend, perhaps a lover.

'Dear Camilla,' he had said, 'I'm writing this while someone makes a boring speech and before I get up to make *my* speech. Will you come and have dinner with me afterwards?'

Tom was very conventional in some ways and always associated food with pleasure. His courtship had been conducted at a series of expensive meals. It ought to have told her something about Tom, but it had failed to do so. Just as the fact that she had suffered indigestion throughout the time of their short engagement should have told something about her. But apparently it had not. They had each remained firmly rooted in their delicate misconceptions of each other.

So every day in their married life they had moved a little further away from each other instead of a step nearer. Perhaps it often happened. But these were two articulate and alert people. And they were English into the bargain, so naturally it hurt them that with all this going for them they couldn't make it work. In bed and out they seemed to grow farther apart. It was at this time that Camilla had redecorated the bedroom from its old sensuous and feminine style iinto a newer and more masculine one.

This time, it was she and not the dog who jerked to attention. A floorboard in the hall outside had creaked. But old houses do move. She stood up and listened.

She went to the door and opened it. The hall was silent and dark. Dark. Dark although she had switched on the light. The darkness seemed active and alive.

With a sick feeling she drew back into the sitting room and closed the door. Her hands were trembling as she reached for the telephone. Then she remembered that the telephone gave a little warning ring in the hall when you dialled a call and that the man out there would know she was calling for help.

Perhaps aggression was the best attack. Open the door, switch on the light and confront her attacker.

Then to her horror she saw the door opening. It opened a fraction and then stopped. Silver gave a small quiet bark. Quickly, without conscious thought, Camilla put up a hand and flicked off the light switch.

She listened but all was silent. She reached out her hand again to grab the heavy vase which stood on the table by the telephone.

'You come one step nearer me,' she said, 'and I'll scream my head off.'

There was still complete silence.

'Who the hell are you, anyway?' she said, a measure of courage coming back to her. 'And how did you get in?'

Even as she spoke she knew the answer: Jen's voice saying, 'your husband wasn't very careful who he handed out keys to', gave it her.

'You're someone who knew my husband,' she said with sudden knowledge. 'Someone who knows me. God, who are you?'

The thought stiffened her and anger burned in her stomach. She flipped on the light.

It was very much closer than she had realised, standing by her shoulder, its paper face turned to her. She tried to scream, but her throat was immediately constricted by the hands. Soft thick padded hands which pressed deep. And deeper.

Clem and Camilla's cousin Jen met on the stairs. As usual Jenny was hurrying and breathless.

'Hello, Clem,' she said, 'Coming to call?'

'I tried to 'phone Camilla, but she doesn't answer the 'phone.'

'She hates it just now,' said Jenny, fumbling in her bag for the key. 'I'll let you in.'

There was a shrill bark from the stairs above them and then the patter of small paws.

'Silver,' said Jen. 'What are you doing? How did you get out?'

She ran up the stairs, calling to Clem to hurry. The front door stood wide open. Camilla lay face downwards on the floor, her head pointing towards them.

'She's dead,' said Clem. He put his bag down on the floor and knelt beside her.

'No, she's not,' said Jenny sensibly. 'She's breathing. I think she's fainted. She may have banged her head as she fell.' Her fingers were feeling Camilla's head delicately. 'Yes, there's a bump. She's going to be all right, her pulse is good and strong. But we ought to have a doctor.'

'I'll go,' said Clem, running down the stairs.

'Telephone,' called Jenny, but it was no use, Clem was gone.

The doctor came without Clem. Camilla soon came round. Perhaps mild concussion, said the doctor and prescribed rest.

There were two great bruises on her throat, one either side, and these the doctor studied thoughtfully. He examined her throat.

Camilla could not speak. There was no real damage done said the doctor. The dumbness was an hysterical reaction and would pass.

She lay there on her pillows looking straight ahead with great pale eyes while Jen sat gently stroking her hand.

'What did happen, dearest?' she said. 'Try to say. We have to know.'

Camilla stared at her, tears began to fill her eyes. 'Tom,' she said, 'Tom. I should never had had Tom watched. It all started then.'

Tom and Sheila waited to hear the front door shut behind their caller. They stood there frozen into attitudes as if they were playing a children's game.

'He's not going to go,' said Sheila.

'Give him a minute,' said Tom, listening.

'No. I could tell. He's not going. You could see it in his face.' Her voice was rising.

'Sheila.' He was trying to calm her.

'He hasn't finished.'

'That's the door closing now.'

'No,' said Sheila. 'He's back in. He never went. I can hear him.' She sat down at her desk, behind her typewriter and smoothed her hair, as if determined to treat this as business. She drank some water.

'We don't have to put up with this,' said Tom decisively. 'I think he's gone out of his mind. I can throw him out and call the police.'

'No, you can't,' said their visitor from the door. In his hand was a gun which he pointed at them. 'It has ammunition in it.' The slightly formal way of speech was usual with him, slips such as he had made earlier were uncommon.

Tom took a step forward and the gun was waved at him. 'Sit down.' With a foot their intruder dragged forward an upright chair and sat down on it. Tom started to speak. 'Don't say anything. I have to think.' He turned his head so that he could fix his eyes on Sheila. For a moment she met his eyes, then she covered her eyes with her hands.

'Don't cover yourself. You can't do it.'

Sheila moved her hands down and crossed her arms nervously across her chest.

'Stop looking at me,' she said.

'Sheila,' said Tom, in a calming voice.

'Oh, she's right to mind. She feels what I am thinking of . . . you two. Here in this room. It disgusts me.'

'It's not true.'

'How was it? Exciting? Or a let down?'

'Oh, please,' said Sheila.

'Well, *you* tell me then, if he won't.'

'There's nothing to tell.'

'Don't shout. Let her speak for herself. Tell me then, Sheila. Just once and I shan't ask again.'

'Don't say a word, Sheila,' said Tom. 'God knows what he's come here for really. But it must be something to do

with Camilla. I knew she was a friend of yours,' he went
on bitterly. 'But I never knew she'd be as dirty as this. Or
you either. Let me tell you that nothing you get now will
stand up in a court of law.'

'You don't understand,' their false friend shook his head.
'I want to shrive your souls.' He took out a cigarette and
sat there smoking it, the ash falling to the floor beside him.
'Someone has to. Or that's my guess.'

'Put that gun, which is only a joke, away, and get out.'

'No joke. I have to keep you here with something.' A
small clod of earth dropped from his shoe to the floor and
was not at first noticed. When he did notice it, he picked
delicately at another piece still sticking to his sole and then
let it fall through his fingers to the ground. Tom watched.

Once one summer evening Sheila and Tom had drawn
close together. They were studying a map of the constituency where there was a lot of re-building.

'That's one of your best streets,' Sheila had said, pointing. 'You polled nearly 100 per cent there. And it's coming
down.'

The front door locked. Their evening work was almost
over. No more visitors were expected.

'Oh, roll it up,' said Tom, 'and let's forget votes. Have
a drink?' He went to the cupboard and produced a bottle.
'Two drinks. One each. That's how I feel.'

'Your wife?' said Sheila cautiously; she believed Tom to
be still in love with his wife. But she accepted the drink.

'You can call her Camilla.'

'Camilla,' said Sheila, sipping her drink. It was gin, far
too strong, but she would have drunk fiercer drinks for
Tom. She was about to do so.

'You know my voice never broke till I was eighteen,'
said Tom. 'I thought I was going to be a freak.'

'Oh Tom.'

'Now when I told Camilla that she didn't even answer.
I suppose she thought there was nothing worth mention-
ing.'

He put his hand on hers; their eyes met. 'I could unlock

the door and we could go home,' said Tom. 'Unless you think it's undignified drinking with your boss.'

'I'm not in a hurry,' said Sheila carefully.

But she was wrong. They were both in a hurry. They were hungry, and for a moment they were both gluttons. It was a warm summer evening and they were both in a hurry.

Just once.

The memory of that one episode weakened him now, when he should act fast.

For the moment both eyes and gun had been off Tom and Tom knew he ought to have rushed him then. With a sickening feeling he realised he had lost his moment. He began to sweat.

'You're a very good girl, Sheila, in some ways, but you don't bring luck to the men you love.'

'She doesn't love me,' cried Tom.

'Doesn't she? Don't you, Sheila? Is that for the record?' Sheila dropped her eyes.

'There you are, you see. I know her better than you do. Tell me, was it good between you and him, Sheila? Have you got that at least to look back on? How was it?'

A fly buzzed at the window and then came circling into the centre of the room.

'It was lovely,' faltered Sheila.

'Sheila!' Tom protested. 'She doesn't know what she's saying.' He felt his fury rising. 'God, I'd like to wipe that smile off your face.'

'Not so good for you then?' An eye was cocked in Tom's direction. 'Rather hasty here, I should think.'

'You're crazy.' But it wasn't craziness. The voice was utterly impersonal. He was only an agent.

'And her too?' This time the gaze went to Sheila, who was trembling.

'Tell Camilla to go to hell.'

'Camilla? Why should you think this has anything to do with Camilla? Perhaps I'm here on my own.'

'I don't believe she can know the way you're acting,'

said Tom, puzzled and fiercely alarmed. He looked at the door. He would have to make for it soon. 'You'll get no evidence this way.'

'If you won't show me the way it is with you, Sheila,' said the visitor, 'I must get you to act it out for me.' He looked directly at Sheila. 'Take your blouse off, Sheila. Ah now, don't mind me, remember I'm only the audience. You're not the only one that knows about audience reaction Tom, remember. I'm in the business too.'

Sheila had obeyed him, in spite of a sound of protest from Tom.

'Now you, Tom. Let's play strip poker. Don't hesitate. Can't you see it's for the best. Get it over quickly. After all, you've taken off your jacket already.'

He turned to Sheila. 'Not cold, are you? It's hot in here. Now your skirt. *Now your skirt!*' As she didn't move. 'Come on, dear, don't think I'm getting a kick out of it. This is strictly business.'

'Don't do it, Sheila,' shouted Tom. 'He wants some sort of evidence. In a moment he'll produce a camera.'

'Now it's your turn. Shirt and trousers off.' He pointed the gun. 'Let's get moving.'

'I'm going to put my coat back on.'

The gun was pointed at Sheila.

'You'd never shoot,' said Tom contemptuously.

'I could nick her a bit. Plastic surgery's not all that good. Not with the breasts.' The coarseness was showing again. Sheila moaned.

'If *you* won't co-operate, *she* will.'

'I'll kill you for this,' said Tom. But he began to obey instructions. He didn't meet Sheila's eyes. He felt demeaned, humiliated, and he knew this was what the man was aiming at.

At one point the man went over to Sheila and helped her remove her thin silk slip. Some of the dirt on his hands removed itself on to her skin. She rubbed at it unhappily with her fingers. She sagged in the chair. Tom felt his flesh sticking wetly to his chair.

The man stood up; he too was breathing heavily. Still looking at them, he withdrew backwards to the door.

'Don't say anything,' he said harshly. 'Don't try to stop me going.'

The door closed. They were alone.

'He's gone,' said Sheila.

'I don't know,' said Tom, still listening. 'I just don't know.'

An insect was buzzing round the centre light. Sheila moved towards the window as if to close it against the entrance of any more. There was a line of sweat on her face. She sat down and put a hand to her head.

'My dear,' said Thomas, turning back to her.

'I'm sorry.' She put her head right down. 'I feel sick.'

'I'm sorry, terribly sorry to have involved you in all this.'

'No. Not you, it's me,' she mumbled. 'Don't you see that? No.' She sat up.

'Are you feeling faint?' He moved to her side.

'No, it's my hands. They've got dirt on them.'

The front door banged again. They both heard it.

'Don't say anything,' said Thomas. 'Don't, don't say anything.'

17

'Kelly's discharged himself from hospital and is on the loose again,' said Dove. 'He came out last night.'

'Did he attack Mrs. Barr, do you think?'

'She isn't accusing him. She's had twenty-four hours to think about it.'

'He has strong feelings about her.'

'There's no evidence anyone was there. The cousin and the man Clem Groves were there soon afterwards and saw nothing. And it wasn't Berkeley. He was home and had a quiet night.'

'Do you think she imagined it all?"

'That or a ghost.' Coffin shrugged. 'She was in an hysterical state. Get a policewoman to go round and have a look at her. Send the Eames girl. God knows she's heavy footed and far from tactful but I've noticed women talk to her.'

Joan Eames was not grateful for the task. She was due to go off duty and was looking forward to going home and washing her hair. She scowled when her superior officer told her what was waiting for her.

'Look, I'm free . . .' she said fiercely. 'And I need that wash. I'm itching. I brought in the Tekel twins who'd been on the loose for three weeks and they were lousy. I itch. I probably smell. I must wash my hair.' She scratched it vigorously.

'Give it a good comb,' said the other heartlessly. 'The boss says move. What does he care if you give lice to Mrs. Camilla Barr?'

'Lice don't fly, they crawl, dear,' said Joan Eames sourly. 'I won't give Camilla Barr lice. I won't touch her.'

'You might, at that,' said the other. 'The boss wants you to get a good look at her throat—bruises and all.'

Joan bared her teeth and made a noise suspiciously like a snarl. She had never heard a noise like it coming from her mouth before and she was surprised to know she could do it. It cheered her up, and she embarked on her interview with a swagger.

Mrs. Barr opened the door herself.

'How are you feeling?' asked Joan.

'Better.'

'It's good of you to see me.'

Camilla shrugged.

'He sent me round to see if I could help. If you'd like me to stay around.' She had decided on this story, hoping fervently that Camilla Barr would say no.

'No,' said Camilla Barr; almost *too* promptly Joan Eames thought. She felt annoyed. Her head itched and she gave it an unobtrusive scratch.

'It was a bad experience,' she said, testing the ground. 'Must have given you a scare.'

'More than that,' said Camilla coolly. 'Much more. I was nearly killed.'

'Your throat?' Joan stared at it hard. 'Does it still give you trouble? Your voice seems all right.'

'It came back quite suddenly.'

'Oh?' Joan considered this. She gave her arm a vigorous scratch.

'Anything worrying you?' said Camilla.

'Just a little irritation.'

'Come and have some tea,' said Camilla. 'I was just going to have some. I can't turn you away from the door, can I?'

Her voice was jerky—tense, over-excited, Joan thought. 'I could do with a cup.'

It was China tea, of course. Lapsang Souchong, pale and fragrant. Joan liked tea to be Indian and strong, with sugar. However, she sipped the tea and watched Camilla and talked.

'I feel better now,' said Camilla with a smile, as she rose to go. 'Thank you for coming.'

'She's in a state, all right,' reported Joan on the telephone. 'I can't make out whether she really was attacked or not. It could be all hysteria.'

When she got home she took out a fine comb and combed her thick hair through. 'Here, have a look,' she said to her sister with whom she lived. 'I itch to death. What is it?'

Her sister looked. 'Nothing,' she said in a crisp tone. 'Scalp's as clean as a whistle. Just nerves. Your imagination.'

Just as Joan got her hair nicely wet and lathered the telephone rang.

'Kelly's been seen in his office,' reported Dove later that evening. 'He's crawling round, but apart from that he's acting normally. Normally for him that is. He tried to call on Mrs. Barr, but she wouldn't see him. I can't imagine him attacking her. No, I don't really see him as a killer. Although he might do anything if pushed. And I don't know why he doesn't have a haemorrhage and die on the spot.'

'He's as strong as an ox, that's why. And obstinate. That helps. Have him watched. And Mark Berkeley too. Anything there?'

'Oh, I've got young Eames working on him. I thought a woman might do a better job. Just put her on it.'

'She's having a busy day,' said Coffin. He went to the window and looked down on the street. It was a fine evening. The shops were still open and people were coming and going. Seen from high up, it looked a busy, cheerful world. 'I'm having a busy day and, come to think of it, there's lots of other busy little people here. Must be.'

He spoke with feeling. In the last twenty-four hours his area had endured a major fire with a robbery; a case of violent assault; three break-ins, one after the other, obviously by the same hands, and a succession of small violent crimes, not all of which had yet come to the notice of the police. One or two never would. The child who had been beaten by her elder sister would never tell the police, even although the fingers of her left hand had been broken in a fall; the grandmother whose grandson had sneaked into her kitchen and stolen her savings would never be allowed to report it. Nor had Coffin yet heard that an unknown person had entered Mark Berkeley's room and attacked one object there. Nobody knew yet except Mark.

Joan Eames, her hair in a turban of red wool, and her temper hot to match, trudged behind Mark, who was wandering from stall to stall in the street market by the Blue Anchor. It was a favourite local shopping place. He didn't seem to be shopping for food as he passed rapidly through the area devoted to fish stalls then the space where all the fruit and vegetable traders shouted and called. For some reason that Joan had never discovered all the fruit and vegetable vendors cried out what they had for sale whereas the fish men kept quiet. It was all right to call out fine potatoes but not fresh haddock. Probably it went back to the ways of mediaeval markets if you could really trace it. Customs cling on in this part of the world, much more than you'd think.

Mark had swung left and moved towards what Joan called the 'shoddy' stalls where luggage and handbags and stuffed toys and dolls were sold. He stopped at one stall and studied it carefully.

Unobtrusively Joan moved up behind him. He wasn't buying luggage anyway; he was looking at the dolls and toys. A nasty lot they looked too, thought Joan. It always amazed her that although the quality of the food sold here was first class, the manufactured objects were both second rate and expensive. Yet they sold. On every side apparently hard-headed housewives, who seemed to know the value of every penny when it came to food, were paying out good money for badly designed and nastily coloured chattels. Either they had no standards about such things or there was something in the noisy, gay atmosphere of the market that aroused extravagance.

Mark hadn't found what he wanted at this stall and he moved off. Joan followed. The stall owners knew her and watched her silently from behind their piled goods. They would ignore her if they could; what they didn't know about wouldn't hurt them.

Mark stopped in front of the biggest and brightest stall there, which belonged to a large blonde called Muriel. She had inherited it from her parents.

'Hello, Dad,' said Muriel brightly. She loved her job. 'Can I help?'

Mark looked at her sourly and in this Joan Eames sympathised with him: who wanted to be Muriel's Dad?

Joan pretended to examine a large pink teddy bear with bright pink eyes. The eyes were very very slightly slanted. British made, a label said. Good old Hong Kong, she thought.

Mark had picked up a doll and was reading the label on it. Silently he handed the doll over to Muriel.

'Oh, is that the one you want, dear? Sure? I mean take your time . . .'

Still silently he handed over the money and waited for the doll.

'Oh, all right, don't say anything,' said Muriel. 'No need to be rude.'

When Mark had walked away, Joan Eames went over and looked at the dolls. They were large and vacant eyed. She read the label. *Talking Doll* it said.

Mark had found his doll and he carried it home in triumph. His bearing was dogged. So was that of Joan Eames, who was still following. He went home; she went after him.

He disappeared inside the house and she stood outside hesitating. Then she followed him into the hall. The door of this house stood always ajar. The young inhabitants were constantly coming and going. But no one was around now. There was a pile of luggage in the hall labelled Wolf. This she nearly fell over.

Joan stood there listening for a moment. All she could hear was Mark labouring up the stairs and then the bang of his door. Her hair felt sticky and damp. She sneezed.

'Oh well, he's safely home,' she said to herself. 'I'll just report in.'

She didn't hear his door lock and even if she had it would have meant nothing much to her. It was such an ordinary sound. She might have worried more, but raised her eyebrows at the sound of the bolt being slipped.

Mark's landlady heard and made a worried noise. 'Bolting the door again. We shall have an accident. Smoking in bed or something and burning us all up, that's what'll happen. I don't like it.'

Mark was quiet behind his locked and bolted door, shut up inside there with his dummy Charlie Grinling and his new doll who could talk.

A little later, Clem came for his usual call. He met Mrs. Jolly on the stairs. 'Oh, you won't get much out of him tonight. Lost his voice.'

'Has he?'

'Yes, wearing a great scarf round his neck. A chill, I suppose. Looks rotten. Don't go in. I shouldn't.'

'I believe I will,' said Clem.

'Please yourself.'

Clem looked at the heap of luggage. 'Someone leaving?'

'My American visitor. It's been a real pleasure to have him. Such an educated boy. He's going home. Back to New York. Winging off tonight. He says his work here is done. And he's had a good time. Isn't that nice?'

'Very,' said Clem.

'I like people to enjoy themselves. And express their pleasure. That's manners, that is. He says he might go to Germany next. His people came from there originally. A long while ago, of course.'

'I'll go on up,' said Clem.

'If you must.'

'I must.'

'You'll have to knock,' called Mrs. Jolly after him. 'He's got it bolted.' She added, 'I don't think he's too well, as a matter of fact.'

'No?'

'It's his voice again.'

'What's wrong with it, then?' said Clem.

'It comes and goes. Since his stroke he's had nothing but trouble with it. Any strain seems to go straight to his vocal chords. Well, it's understandable, isn't it? When your voice is all important to you, as his has been to him, *that's* where the strain is going to show up, isn't it?'

Clem nodded.

He walked slowly up the stairs. He knocked on the door and waited for it to open.

'Come on,' he said, rattling the door. 'Let me in.'

The door opened and Mark stood there. He was a tall man. Taller than Clem by about four inches, and much broader.

'Hurt your throat?' said Clem.

Mark silently shook his head.

'Throat giving you any discomfort?' Clem tried again. He was genuinely puzzled. For the life of him he couldn't see why Mark's throat should be giving him any trouble. 'Well, say something.'

Mark produced a piece of paper on which was printed large: CAN'T TALK.

'Oh.' Clem nodded. 'Well, I'd better go away again. Yes, better all round.' He turned to depart, but Mark put his hand firmly on his shoulder. 'Oh, go on,' said Clem. 'Let go or I'll shout.'

The grip increased if anything.

'So all right, I wouldn't shout.' Clem turned back into the room. 'What is it you want? No lesson today, Mark. You've lost your voice. We can't do anything.'

Mark released his grip and pointed to a chair. Clem sat down obediently. The dummy, Charlie Grinling, also wearing a scarf, sat opposite.

'No more lessons, though, Mark,' Clem said. 'I'm giving notice. No more lessons.' He looked at Mark. 'Well, don't you think we did enough? You gave me a good voice production, Mark. I'll say that for you.'

Mark went over to the cupboard where he kept his dummy and got out a bottle and two glasses. The doll from the market slipped out of the cupboard and on to the floor.

'Whisky? No, thanks. You know I don't go for that. You collecting dolls now, Mark?' Clem pointed.

Mark tapped his throat.

'Yes, I suppose it will help your throat. You have it by yourself.'

Obstinately Mark poured two glasses. Clem sighed. 'I don't understand about your throat,' he said.

Mark produced his bit of paper and wrote in large block capitals: BRUISED.

'Oh.' He looked carefully at Mark. 'Do it yourself?'

Mark shook his head.

'Someone attack you then?'

Again Mark shook his head.

'Have you told the police?'

Another shake of the head from Mark.

'Have you been to the doctor then?'

Mark picked up his piece of paper. NO NEED, he wrote.

Clem stood up to go. 'Thanks for the drink, Mark. I didn't enjoy and I didn't want it, and, if you noticed, I didn't drink it, but thanks all the same.' Unconsciously he was treating Mark as if he was deaf as well as temporarily dumb.

Mark stood in his way to the door and Clem hesitated. 'Let me see that throat of yours.' He put up a quick hand whisked the scarf away. The throat was clear and unblemished, the skin slightly flushed but not bruised. 'There's nothing wrong with *your* throat.'

Mark tucked the scarf back making a neat job of it. Then he went over to Charlie Grinling and unwound the scarf round his neck.

There was a great ragged scar across the calico throat, sewn up with big black stitches. Mark made a quick vivid gesture with his hand, miming the throat cutting operation.

'So Charlie's had his throat cut,' said Clem. 'When you can't talk, he can't talk, and when he can't talk, then you can't talk. I get it. It's a bomb.'

'Wouldn't it be fun,' said Charlie, in a light treble, 'if you were a doll like me?'

'God,' said Clem, stepping back.

'I wish you and I were friends,' said Charlie.

Clem backed away further, knocking over a small table and tumbling the lamp to the ground. It went out.

'My eyes are magic, I can see in the dark.'

Clem, fumbling round to find the light switch by the door, gave the doll a kick as he passed with his long legs.

'You're my best friend in the whole world,' said Charlie.

Clem found the light switch and pushed it on. 'God,' he said. Mark was sitting on the edge of the bed looking at him. 'What a thing a to do.'

'Wouldn't it be fun if you were a doll like me,' said Charlie hurriedly.

'I'll kill you,' said Clem, throwing a glass at him.

'I wish you and I were friends.'

'Shut up.' The glass missed.

'My eyes are magic and I can see in the dark.' Apparently there was a bit more to come, and eventually Charlie made it: 'Can you?' he finished up triumphantly.

'No, I bloody well can't,' said Clem.

Mark was still sitting on the bed and Clem turned to him. 'Someone tears the dummy's throat out to stop you talking. Very right and proper in my opinion. You've replaced his so-called vocal cords with a doll's jaw box. You're crackers. You shouldn't have done it.'

'Someone was you,' said Mark in a thick voice.

'Now you can talk.'

'My eyes are magic,' said Charlie, Clem pushed the dummy back into the chair and it now went quiet. There were faint clicks inside which suggested that the mechanism was still trying to work.

'It has to come back some time.'

'That I don't see. Silence is golden they say.' Clem sounded quite cocky, but edgy.

'Have much to say to you,' said Mark slowly.

'Well, we'll soon fix that,' said Clem. 'If cutting the doll's throat shuts you up, I can get to work on it now.'

'No use,' said Mark. 'Could only work once. Shock. Better now.'

'Better now,' mimicked Clem. 'It's you that needs voice production now. Or voice protection,' he added thoughtfully.

'No joke,' said Mark.

'Not a joke at all. Nothing is a joke. What was it we did to each other, Mark, that was so funny? I never laughed. I came here to you regularly and we had a relationship. You were the teacher and I was the pupil. You taught and I listened. I followed my instructions. Don't think I didn't know what you were doing to me, Mark.'

'We both knew,' said Mark. 'It was a conversation, not a dialogue.'

'You wanted someone to kill Tom and Sheila for you. You thought I was the person to do it. You gave me your instructions when I came for my lessons. Because you didn't have the physical strength to do it. You can hardly use your right hand, can you? I suppose you thought it was a sort of hypnotism, Mark. But it wasn't hypnotism. You couldn't make me do what I didn't want to do. I went along with you because I wanted. It wasn't hypnotism but symbiosis, Mark. We were getting nourishment from each other.'

'Of course you wanted to kill Tom. And shame him. I knew that. For the love we bore Phil Daly.'

'I bore him more than you did,' said Clem sharply.

'That's disputable.'

'Well, who did the killing? That proves who cared more. I cared most. It was I that went out and redeemed Phil's lovely masculinity that they ruined.'

'He was mine,' said Mark. 'He was much more mine than yours. It was me he loved.'

'You were a father figure, that's all. I was his equal. More,' said Clem fervently. 'When I had to be, I was his willing slave, and *vice versa*. That's what you can't stand.'

'We both loved him. I admit that.'

'Yes, but with you it was more in the way of business. He'd been part of your act. When he married that woman, a part of your image went with him. She misled him terribly about his real nature. We all know that. She shamed him. And then making love to Tom Barr behind his back. Well, I shamed her in her turn.'

'I loved him.'

'But let's get this straight. You may have taught me something, but I have been the principal mover. That's a revelation to you, isn't it? You don't like to believe that, do you?'

'It's not true.'

'You want to think it's all you. You can't bear to think that I should have loved more than you did. Or that he loved me more. Or that I did more for him. That's what's eating you up. That's why you lost your voice.'

'I lost my voice because you wounded Charlie. Because you were jealous.'

'Jealous? Me? Of a dummy? Of you with a dummy? You want your head examined.'

'My head has been examined,' said Mark in a low voice, 'and found wanting.'

'What we had as a relationship was good and real. Authentic. But only because that was the way I wanted it. Let's be clear about it.'

'My poor boy,' began Mark.

'I don't know what poor boy you're talking about.'

'Phil.'

'He was no more yours than Sheila's. He's nobody's now.'

'Nothing always comes down to nothing in the end.'

'What are you mouthing about?'

'You failed with Kelly and Camilla Barr. They're not dead.'

'I'm not cut out for a mass murderer. I did Sheila and Tom—that was punishment. That was right. I had some hate there.'

'And you had the gun,' said Mark. 'It's easy to kill with a gun. Here's the gun again.' He produced it from a pocket and threw it on the bed.

'No, it's not easy,' said Clem, not looking at the gun.

'How could you say that? It's never easy. You have to work yourself up. Sort of masturbation.'

'I always wondered what you did that night you killed them,' said Mark.

On that night that they died, Tom and Sheila heard the door click for the second time and knew that their attacker had come back.

Thomas smiled at Sheila to give her courage. He thought he knew what was coming. 'Put something on,' he said wanting to face his death with dignity. Half remembered in his mind was the earlier smile he had given her. Between a smile and a smile a gulf opens.

'Don't say anything,' he said. 'Don't, don't say anything.'

Sheila went running forward to meet Clem as she heard him coming. She took the first shot.

Then Clem raised the gun and shot Thomas Barr.

This part was all over in two minutes.

The whole episode had been completed within half an hour.

18

When Coffin was told that Mark was in his room, he nodded. 'Let him be for the moment. Thanks,' he said to Joan Eames and smiled. I suppose he thinks the smile makes up for all, she thought cynically, her wet hair was souring her temper. It'll look frizzled as hell, she thought.

On his desk was the paper mask that had been found in the rubbish bin in the old cemetery. He threw it across the table to her.

'See that smear on the back? We think it's make-up.'

'Looks like it,' said Joan.

'Do you make anything of it? Is that a man's cosmetic? Or a woman's?'

'Contrary to what you might think,' said Joan, 'there is no difference. Even the colour tones don't differ all that much. Plenty of women have dark skins. This isn't all that dark, as a matter of fact.'

'That's what I thought,' said Coffin, withdrawing the mask. 'If it was a man where would he use a colour like this?'

'On the upper cheeks, I suppose,' said Joan studying him, 'towards the nose or on the forehead . . . that's where the skin is palest on a man.'

'Thanks,' said Coffin.

'I don't know what he'd use it for, though,' said Joan. 'What kind of a man uses make-up?'

'You're not using your imagination,' said Coffin. 'Why do you use it?'

'To look better,' said Joan without hesitation.

'That's it,' said Coffin. 'To look better. It's the universal idea, isn't it?'

Joan looked at him suspiciously.

'You wonder what I'm getting at, don't you?'

Joan was silent. Prolonged speech with her superior did not come her way very much and she wasn't sure how to handle it. 'No, I see what you're getting at,' she said. 'It could be used to cover a blemish or a scar.'

'And who has a scar? You know that too?'

She shook her head. It wasn't a conversation, she now realised. He was talking to himself.

'Clem Grove. He must have a scar. He had a birthmark removed. We don't see anything but it must be there. All that's left after they finished plastic surgery. A scar covered with make-up.'

'You haven't finished yet,' he said to Joan Eames. 'Take a man with you and go and call on Clement Grove. Make an excuse and look at his face hard. Tell me if you see make-up.'

'I might not recognise it,' said Joan.

'You will. It's your job to recognise it. And when you've done that, go round and knock Mark up and see his make-up. Then ring me.'

Joan went to the Museum which was shut and dark. Then she went to where Clem lived in a suburb which ran to the west of Exhibition Street. Clem lived in an Edwardian block of flats due to be demolished next year. The contractors already had a board up as if they couldn't wait to start making holes.

She rang and got no answer. Finally, a little out of turn, she rang John Coffin and said she was on her way round to Mark Berkeley.

'I don't like it here,' she said. 'There's something wrong here.'

What she had got was what astronomers call a displacement effect. She could sense a disturbance somewhere but she couldn't quite work out where it was coming from. It was a sort of emotional Doppler effect, indicating Mark as the probable source of the disturbance but she couldn't be sure.

Afterwards when she was asked to say what gave her this idea all she could point to were small things.

A milk bottle still on Clem's doorstep, uncollected since the morning. A letter pulled from the box, read on the spot and then thrown away as if the recipient had been in a great hurry. A curtain at the window, half drawn.

'That's being a detective,' said Coffin when she told him.

It's being a woman, she thought, but did not say. Equal work for equal pay, she added sardonically.

Mark and Clem and the dummy made three.

'So that's how it was,' said Mark as he listened to the end of Clem's story. 'I suppose I guessed. You've never had any self control. Could never have been a performer. I'll let you into a secret: your voice production is still rotten. It never could improve. You haven't got it in you, boy. Why, I could do more with that surly copper that keeps hanging about. Or that big-footed girl who thought I didn't see her in the market.'

'Your nastiness is a constant revelation to me,' said Clem.

'I meant it to be an execution and you turned it into an orgy.'

'Don't use words like that,' said Clem coldly.

'And yet you must have got the idea from me somehow, seeing the whole *idea* was mine. Yet how? I swear I do not see.'

'Don't kid yourself,' said Clem. 'Ideas are given to all of us.'

'But where do they come from?' said Mark softly. 'All these ideas, where do they come from? Someone gives us them.'

The ceaseless pressure of one mind on another. That is the real source of murder, but neither said so.

'Some people round here think the ghost of old Isaiah Steinberg has been at work,' said Clem. 'But you and I know better.'

'I guess the police know better too,' said Mark. 'I suppose they're after you. I doubt if you're very clever about it all, from what you say.'

'They haven't a clue,' said Clem.

'You can't act, you know,' said Mark. 'Never could,

never will. Poor performer. What's not there can't be built in. You gave yourself away, I expect. Not that it matters.'

'I shall make a full confession,' said Clem. 'It was a crime of passion. They'll understand. That's their job.'

'They don't understand everything. They won't understand I was using you like my Charlie here.' He gave Charlie a slap and set him upright. 'I hated Thomas Barr who helped get rid of the old Regency Theatre. They *loved* me there. I'd still have been a name but for him. I hated Sheila who took away my Phil, whom I loved like a lover. It seemed to me right you should be the killer. So I groomed you.'

'Thanks for electing me,' said Clem.

'I chose you because I thought, I have always thought, that it was you that killed Phil. That he didn't commit suicide but that you murdered him.'

Clem flushed and then went white.

'So that was what was in my mind. Then too, although you will never be a performer, my dear, you are a good subject. Not for hypnotism. I don't use the word. More a kind of telepathy such as existed between Charlie and me.' Again he touched the dummy, whose arms fell forward. 'One mind can rest heavily upon another. Don't think I don't know it. But where did the dirt get in, that's what I wanted to know.'

'I feel perfectly free,' said Clem. 'Stop working me up. My God, it's impossible to talk to you.'

'I'm a rain-maker, a medicine man,' said Mark. 'I could knock spots off that old quack round the corner who pretends to cure my rheumatism. The thoughts I've had about him.'

'You are crackers,' said Clem simply and with emphasis.

'For some time now I've been trying to make you see what I wanted from you. But you haven't got the message.'

'Don't push me,' said Clem.

'You attacked my poor little Charlie here. As if *he* counted.' Mark laughed.

'My God, I'll kill you.' Clem picked up the gun from the bed.

'Ah now you've got the message,' said Mark triumphantly. 'That's what I wanted. Be my docile murdering doll.'

The shot, fitted with a silencer, made hardly a sound. Mark received the shot in his head. It entered one eye. Only the doll spoke.

'Wouldn't it be fun if you were a doll like me. I wish you and I were friends. My eyes are magic. I can see in the dark. You are my best friend in the whole world,' said Charlie rapidly.

Joan Eames was banging on the door.

'My best friend,' said Charlie. 'My best friend, my best friend.'

'You've left me nothing to do except clear up,' said Coffin to Joan Eames. She wasn't sure if this was praise or censure.

'The doctor gave Clement Grove a shot. He was in a terrible state. I don't know why he killed Mark. I think the old man must have needled him into it. That's how he stands. Anyway, he wants to talk. He wants to confess to killing Thomas Barr and Sheila Daly whom he says he wished to kill. And attacking Camilla Barr and Martin Kelly whom he says he didn't wish to kill. I believe him. He says he was going to confess anyway. I believe that too.'

'And what did you make of him? You were first in here, you saw the scene. What sort of scene was it?'

'I don't think Clement Grove had planned to kill Mark Berkeley. A quarrel blew up and the gun was there.'

'Why was the gun there?'

'I think Mark Berkeley must have left it around himself.'

'On purpose?'

'I couldn't tell that. I'd guess so. The gun must have been common property, kept here for safe keeping. It was used on Barr and Daly, then again on Kelly.'

'They hadn't been doing much drinking. No sign of drugs. No real sign of a brawl. A glass on the floor. It looked as though Clement just picked up the gun and let him have it. There was only one shot.'

'I'm told there was only one shot left in it. It was also the gun that killed Barr and Daly.'

'And yet it was in Berkeley's possession and not Clem Grove's.' Joan frowned.

'They were in it together. Must have been.'

'I suppose it'll all be in Grove's statement,' said Joan Eames.

Coffin laughed. 'If that clears the whole thing up then it will be the first time any statement ever did. There'll be questions that never get answered.'

Joan Eames was silent. She felt a little sick and tired. Death on an empty stomach was no treat to her.

'Funny, I had it down that Mark Berkeley was the killer.'

'You'll get it straight,' said Joan sympathetically. And what she also meant was: and I can get off home.

'There's always some things left that you don't understand,' said Coffin.

He looked in a puzzled way round the room, still redolent of Mark. The overcoat he had worn that evening to go to the market, the bottle of whisky by the bed, the faint scent from the cologne that he always wore. On the chair was Charile Grinling and on the floor was the now speechless talking doll.

Coffin straightened Charlie Grinling and patted his head. 'What a story you could tell, eh boy, if you could really talk.'

When the crowd of policemen and photographers and technicians had cleared the room, Coffin was left alone in it for a moment. It wasn't usual for him to be last at the scene of a crime. With his rank he was usually away leaving the routine to go forward without him.

That was the way it went: the better you were as a detective, the less detection you ended up doing. Instead, you ended up reading reports and dictating your own. He said this aloud often, and half believed it, but he knew it wasn't entirely true. In the end, the flair was his. And although patience and detailed work on routine matters brought in the information, it was his mind that analysed and saw the right connections.

He looked around the confusion of the room and saw that it reflected the atmosphere of the whole case. And yet still some mystery remained.

'I know what happened here. I know now what happened in Tom Barr's office. But what was truly behind it all? I don't feel I shall ever know that.'

He shut the door behind him and walked down the stairs. Mrs. Jolly met him at the bottom. She appeared calm.

'How are the boys?' he asked, knowing that this would be her chief worry.

'I'm shipping most of them out tomorrow. One group are going on tour, another set are moving to be near the film studio, to start shooting. They've only been learning the dance routines up here. New intake not due to arrive until after the weekend. By that time you'll be out of here?'

'Try to be.'

'So for a while I'll have an empty house.' She sounded sad. 'Mark gone. And my favourite lodger off back to America.' She opened the front door for him. 'Even the street lighting is depressing me these days. They're changing over to a different system. Seems darker to me, had you noticed?'

Coffin went out into the street. 'It's a funny business. Why did Mark set up this apparatus for revenge? Who was really scoring off who? Where did it all come from?'

It had been a long day and he was tired. One task remained. Not one he looked forward to doing. 'I ought to call on Camilla Barr. She can't be left just to read about it in the newspapers. Someone's got to tell her all there is to tell. I suppose I could have sent Joan Eames. But no, they don't like each other. Not that Eames said, but I could read between the lines. Eames is a good girl.'

He walked round to where Camilla lived in Tom Barr's old apartment. He looked up at her window and could see a light shining. She was home.

'I could ring the bell and go on up now.' He glanced down the road and saw a figure approaching. He watched with interest and even some amusement.

Camilla was waiting for an event which she guessed must take place. No one had told her it was going to happen, it was an event to which her own reactions were as yet unpredictable. She would not know how she was going to feel until it had happened to her. It was like a surgical operation about which you feel brave but ignorant.

But an observer might have thought that not only did she look forward to what was coming but that she knew when it was going to happen.

She was preparing for it. In her own way, not even Camilla could deny that she was making ready. Whether she liked it or not, her body was doing it for her. Skin, eyes, lips were ready before she was. But she caught up, joined in, put on some lipstick, sprayed Cabuchard on her hair and smoked a cigarette. Scent and cigarette smoke mixed are powerfully disturbing.

When the door bell rang, she answered it at once.

'Hello,' she said to Martin Kelly, 'I've been expecting you.'

'I telephoned once but you didn't answer.'

'No. I was here though. I heard it ring. I just sat and listened to it ring. I knew it was you.'

They regarded each other silently.

'We've been in the wars. Both of us.' Gently she put a hand on his cheek. 'Sore?'

He shook his head.

'Say something. Anything.'

'Camilla.'

'Yes, that'll do to start with.'

'Camilla.'

'What liars we've been to each other. And without using words, either.' Of the two, Camilla was always going to be the more articulate. She would always tell them exactly what was or was not in their relationship, sometimes hurrying them forward prematurely, sometimes putting in speech what was better left unsaid. It was what had killed her with Tom.

'I don't think I've lied to you, Camilla.'

'It wasn't very sensitive of me to ask you to watch Tom.'

'But I didn't tell you any lies on him.'

'You know why I did it?' said Camilla.

'I thought you wanted me to know. And I thought there was something positive about that. That you wanted me to know Tom was unfaithful and you were going to take action. That's what I thought at first. Till he was killed and I saw who his caller was. You knew that man, Camilla.'

'It was he who telephoned me in New York, telling me about Tom and Sheila, making it sound like dirt.'

'To him it was dirt. The way he's built it was dirt, indeed.'

'You thought he and I conspired to kill Tom,' cried Camilla.

Kelly spread out his hands. 'I thought maybe you wanted me to do it for you. Then I thought you wanted me to bear witness that you could not have been there. I hated you then.'

'You made that clear. At least you never went off the boil one way or another. I think I'd have hated that more.'

'You *are* cold-blooded, Camilla.'

She shook her head silently and smiled. 'You came crawling out of hospital to see me, didn't you?'

'When I knew you'd been hurt. Read it in the paper. Mrs. Camilla Barr, it said. So it was you.'

'I wasn't really badly hurt. He didn't want to hurt me. He tried, but he couldn't do it. He hurt you, though.' Once again her hand touched his cheek and he caught at it.

'Camilla—when I was crawling round after I was hurt, it was to you that I was crawling. I knew that if I kept going I would get back to you.' He put out a hand. 'I think I've got you, Cam.'

'I didn't stay with Tom because he didn't have the sort of life I wanted to have. You're rough, not sophisticated; I don't think you'll have the sort of life I want either.' She gave a delicious shiver at this source of private joy.

'I won't divorce you, Cam,' he said. 'To begin with I'm a Catholic. And second, I wouldn't anyway.'

'That's how it'll be then,' said Camilla. 'Till death us do part.'

'Don't make that sort of joke, Cam.'

'No. No, I shouldn't. It was bad taste, wasn't it. I feel bad about Sheila Daly. I hated her a little. I shouldn't have done that.'

'I'll tell you something I've discovered about her. The weekend she was killed she'd planned to go to a Retreat at an Anglican Convent. To be quiet and meditate.'

'I think that's sad.'

'It rounds out the picture of her, doesn't it. I think she must have had feelings of guilt too. It's something about her I know and John Coffin doesn't. I'll leave it that way.'

In the street below Coffin had watched Kelly hurry up to Camilla. 'End of a story,' he thought. 'Kelly drove a sort of bargain with me, after all.'

Then he had walked forward. It did seem darker, somehow. Mrs. Jolly was right. Perhaps this darkness was behind the rise in his crime statistics? It was worth considering.

Over a hundred years ago, the youngest son of Isaiah Steinberg had left London and emigrated to America. After a short stay in New York working as a clerk in a dry saltery firm he had moved into Pennsylvania and to the developing industrial area around Philadelphia. He still continued working as a clerk, but this time as a shipping clerk. Later in life, when over forty, he married a Jewish girl of a good family settled for some generations in Pennsylvania. They had two sons and one daughter. He died in 1870. He did not forget his father who had died in faraway pre-Victorian London. His two younger children died young in a typhoid epidemic. The elder boy, better educated than his father, successful and handsome, became a lawyer and rich by the standards of the family. He was an intellectual and, after a short visit to Austria and Poland to visit relations, a convinced believer in social reform. He died in 1917, rather poorer than he had been in earlier life but still breathing revolutionary fire. His only child, a son, was killed in France in 1918 at the age of twenty-six, leaving a widow and an infant daughter who grew up to be a moody restless woman who died by her own hand in 1940. Her son was Joseph Wolf in whom the family history lived and breathed.

The Trans-American flight now bore Joe smoothly over

the Atlantic on its curving yet direct flight north and west. The traveller was tired, but satisfied.

His English trip had not been without results. There had been a mystery, a scandal. Many people would always believe now that professional politicians were discreditable. You could never efface this sort of memory altogether. It hung on, like Mayerling, like the Dreyfus affair, colouring the minds of future generations as yet unborn.

He smiled at the stewardess as she brought him a drink. It was the minds of people like her he aimed at bending. He drank, still smiling.

'My boss in Washington thought I was an Organisation man, *his* man. But I'm not, I'm a Disorganisation man. He'll soon find out. Very soon now. He's the next person I plan to work on. I'm not an anarchist, but I go around preparing the ground for revolution. I planted my British seed in the minds of Berkeley and Clem Groves and it destroyed Tom Barr, and with him a little bit of the British political scene. No, I didn't waste my time there.'

He leaned back and the stewardess watched him. He's got a sweet smile. He looks a happy man. As if he was satisfied. You don't often see a man look like that. She moved away, slightly puzzled and a little envious.

Joe watched her back retreating down the gangway. Nice girl, he thought. And how little she knows what I've been up to, and how little she would understand.

Yes, he was satisfied. He had a situation nicely building up in Washington. His next trip would be to Bonn where he had a new friend called Müller. He was prospecting a situation there. It should develop in time.

This was how you prepared for revolution: by dissolving the old structure of politics.

Far away from this flight Isaiah Steinberg's bones lay in the burying ground for the condemned in the old prison where he had been hung. But in this sense he was stirring in his grave.

A Savage Place

By Robert B. Parker

Called away from his Boston turf, crack detective Spenser
takes on the assignment of protecting Candy Sloan, a glam-
orous Hollywood television reporter on the verge of breaking the biggest story of her career. The glittering storybook
world of Hollywood is laid bare as Candy and Spenser seek
to prove allegations of mob payoffs into the movie business.

"Robert B. Parker continues to write tough private eye
stories with exceptional wit, compassion and intelligence."
$2.95   —The Houston Post